A COLLECTION OF SHORT STORIES

as Written by

the ENERGIZED TURTLE

To Celeste
Enjoy
Love, Jo

JOSEPHINE (JO) LA RUSSA GRAVEN

A Collection of Short Stories

ISBN: 978-1-954693-26-5

FV-9

www.IntellectPublishing.com

Table of Contents

The Energized Turtle ..9
Kaleidoscope 11
Buffalo Roam the Streets of Fairhope 13
Fleeting Gold 23
The Missing Piece 27
How Do You Say, "I Love You?" 29
How I Met My Husband 31
The Refund 36
The Intern 43
The Ghost of Eastern Shore Art Center 51
The Tinker Man 56
Confusing Interpretation 62
Is There Really a Santa Claus? 64
The Memory Quilts 68
Only in My Family 75
Miniature Lighthouse 77
The Blue Bottles .84
The Search for a Bride 90
Larry's Dilemma 97
Avocado Alien 101
The Last Summer Gathering at the River 107
Breaking News 115

Moving Sketches	118
Eavesdropping in the Bar	128
Running Away	131
The Preacher's Sermon	134
I'm Waiting	138
That's Hog-Wash My Darling	143
Christmas Surprise	145
The Prediction	151
The Margarita Girls	155
The Rough Looking Cowboy	162
Aged, but Not Alone	167
Happy	176
Determined to Give and He Gave His All	179
The Leather-Bound Book	181
Sunset at the Pier	187
My Dream Vacation	192
Was Thomas Wolf Right After All? Can You Go Home Again?	196
My Favorite Place to Read	202

Acknowledgement

Barbara Echols is a dear friend who reads what I write and gives me her opinion of what might be a more effective and a clearer presentation of each short story and the collection of stories as a book. I value her editing remarks and her appraisal of the finished collection. Thank you, Barbara, for giving of your time and reaction to this latest writing of mine.

Carolyn Bartle is another dear friend who has read some of these stories through the years. She has helped with proofing and shared her thoughts about the stories. This is a valuable help to me to be a more effective writer. Carolyn shares how she thinks readers might respond to the variety of stories and placement. Thank you, Carolyn, for your many helpful comments and great proofing skills.

Joan Cowles is a very dear friend and former travel buddy. Joan shared that she used to proofread material sent to her husband's printing business and offered to proof for me. I am thrilled that she took the time to read and add her input on the correctness and flow of stories. Thank you, Joan for being a part of my writing team and sharing.

A COLLECTION OF SHORT STORIES
as Written by
the ENERGIZED TURTLE

The Energized Turtle

As a young adult, some compared me to the energized bunny in the commercial who just kept going. I have a type A personality. I determine what I want to accomplish each day and write out my TO DO list. I rarely stop until I have completed it and marked off the tasks.

In my younger days, as a wife and mother of four, a full-time teacher, taking nine graduate hours each quarter at UAB with special permission from the Alabama State Department of Education, a Sunday school teacher, and in two other religious organizations, I had to multi-task. Yes, I cooked a hot breakfast each morning and a full healthy meal each night for supper. I fixed a lunch for my family each work/school day. We all took our lunches. Everybody worked together.

I still make the list and mark it off as I have always done. Some days there are more tasks than usual and I stay up late at night or work through the night to finish. This is especially true when I am writing. My mind won't slow down and I write until the morning light begins to shine in my window. Then I go to sleep until my eyes decide to open.

Until six years ago, I was involved in six church organizations, one professional educators' group, two Bible study groups, a creative writing group, and two social groups. I wrote for my high school alumni quarterly newsletter, and traveled often.

After some major health issues six years ago, I had to cut back. I didn't get my strength back and still haven't. I have a diabetic foot that requires a brace that goes almost to my knee. Thankfully, it is my left foot, so I can drive wherever I wish. It does mean I use a cane and sometimes a walker. Steps, slopes, and high curbs restrict me. I just find another means of going places. After effects of chemotherapy have robbed me of fine motor skills of my hands. Buttoning or zipping clothes create a challenge, as does typing on the computer. I still do my own housework, grocery shopping, and belong to a cooking group, two writing groups, one professional educators' group, one church organization, and two social groups. I entertain in three groups from eight to forty-five guests, and I do all the cooking and baking from scratch for these gatherings. Yes, I have health issues that won't get better, but I don't let them stop me. Like the turtle in Aesop's Fable, **Tortoise and the Hare**, I keep on going, but at a slower pace. I am the seventy-eight- year-old Energized Turtle.

Kaleidoscope

Life is a kaleidoscope, an ever-changing picture. The American College Dictionary gave three definitions for a kaleidoscope. One stated, "It is a small tube in which patterns of color are optically produced and viewed for amusement, especially one in which mirrors reflect light transmitted through bits of loose colored glass contained at one end, causing them to appear as symmetrical designs when viewed at the other."

Life of a person is like that tube. The entire human being is that upright tube, self-contained but with millions of possibilities to choose along life's path. Some are small and seemingly forgotten, but they are small pictures within one's life that trigger another action.

The baby, so unaccustomed to life outside the womb, quickly learns to cry, smile, laugh, babble, crawl, then walk. For the young child, maybe it is the feel of a smooth rock, a bird's song or the tick of a clock that catches his or her attention, and the child looks at the rock and feels it. Maybe he or she puts it in the mouth to explore the taste of dirt or sand on its hard surface. The chirp of the bird causes the picture to shift from rock to the tree above and the child searches for the songster. The tick of the clock on the wall is heard and the focus shifts. The mind races onto the next image.

With each twist of the tube a new image emerges. Each action in life has a reaction that causes yet another, and the process goes on throughout life. The tight picture grows larger with specks of light here and there. The brain at work, exploring, analyzing, and making judgments. The person grows both physically and intellectually. The tight pictures with its darker colors transform the person as understanding occurs, as decisions are made and actions are taken. They cause the image to grow and change, to lighten and darken at the joys and perils of one's life. The loose bits of glass at the end of the kaleidoscope are the events in life. The mirror reflection is the perception of self. Mirrors distort the image at times. The distorted view is what others see. They do not see or understand the internal workings of the being in that body, only a moment's glimpse.

The patters of color are moods: blue-serenity, green-envy, red-passion, yellow-happiness, orange-determination, grey-confusion and doubt, and black-despair. Each comes and goes, ever changing almost every day in some way. Yes, life is a constantly changing set of colors caused by the phases of growing up, encountering and reacting to the endless events along the way.

Buffalo Roam the Streets of Fairhope

"WOW! Willie, listen to this article in today's newspaper. This is it, my gold mine just waiting for me to apply! I already have a trailer and with your dad's help, I am going to be rich, rich, rich!"

"What does it say?"

Willie was hanging over Daniel's shoulder as he read the news clip to him.

"Auburn University Research Center has received a grant to breed buffalo that could be used as an alternative food source that would be lean and tender. Buffalo have been used as a meat source for centuries, but the meat was stringy and tough. The proposal states researchers would crossbreed grain fed cows with buffalo. The restrictive laws of the national parks in Montana, Idaho and Wyoming have a major over-population problem. It is the right time for the proposal to be granted. The federal government has given the university permission to bring 1,000 buffalo to the research farm off County Road 104 and County Road 13. Grazing land is there with grasses studied and improved over the past 10 years. Cattle fed on these grasses gained weight, produced a higher grade of beef and with less body fat. The meat seems to melt in the mouths of the diners at Jesse's. Of course, it could have been the cup of whiskey they poured over each steak. It could have been tender or tough. They were too intoxicated to know after the third bite.

Shipment of buffalo will be staggered over a three-year period. Monthly, 28 buffalo will arrive. The first shipment will be sent in early May by truck transport. The individual hired will be paid $3,000.00 plus all expenses to deliver the buffalo. Applicants need to apply during this week at Suite 298 of the government building on Clay Road."

Daniel threw down the paper, changed his shirt and combed his hair then ran out the door and hopped into his car. The tires were smoking as he peeled out the drive and headed for the government building. He filled out the forms and was hired on the spot.

Now Daniel knew he would have to make at least two trips to get all 28 to Fairhope. The government agent told him the 28 had to be picked up by April 30, and all had to leave the park at the same time. They did not have time to round up a few at a time. That was dangerous work.

Daniel thought about it. If he could modify his trailer to allow for more ventilation and ease in feeding these monsters, he could make the trip in three days. Of course, he'd need a second trailer. His cousin Willie also had a tractor trailer and they would share the money. His Uncle Henry had a machine shop, so he went to see him.

"Uncle Henry, I've been offered a job transporting buffalo to Alabama and if I do it right, I will have one load of buffalo to deliver every month for the next three years. They will pay all expenses and give me $3000.00 for each trip. Now here is the problem. My trailer bed is closed. In three days, they would be dead in that confined area.

Uncle Henry sat down and twisted the cap off two bottles of beer. He handed one to Daniel and he took a swig out of his. His uncle commented: "Sounds like you got a problem, son. What are you going to do about it?"

"That's where you come into the picture."

"Me, Daniel, I am too old and not that darn crazy to haul buffalo around the country. You find you somebody else. What you trying to do kill your old uncle?"

"Hear me out. I don't expect you to drive those buffalo to Alabama. I just need for you to build two special framed trailer beds."

"And what little metal fencing do you plan to put around these trailer beds?"

"Highways have these heavy gauge metal strips reinforced with steel cables to keep cars and trucks from crossing a meridian and killing someone in the oncoming lane. Now I was thinking, if you took our trailer beds and welded those heavy steel posts all around it and then attach those big metal strips to it. It would be sturdy. But to be on the safe side, add rows of steel cable around every 18 inches, it would be strong enough to contain those buffalo. What do you say? Can you do it?"

"How much is in it for me?"

"I'll pay you $1,000. 00 for modifying the trailers. "

"You gettin' $3,000.00 a load and you offering me just $1,000. No way man. I want $2,000.00"

"That means Willie and I only get $500. each and we'd be doing all the hauling."

"Alright, I'll settle for $1,500.00 since my son Willie will be using his trailer."

"It's a deal, but you don't get paid until I make my first run and you only get paid for our first haul."

Uncle Henry went to the junk yard to find steel wiring, and used steel strips. He bought new steel post and the rest of the steel sheeting for the sides. He did his regular orders until five o'clock then worked on the modified beds until his eyes began to droop. He didn't tell Daniel where he'd got his supplies. Once those buffalo got in there, it wouldn't be shiny and new anyway. He took one of the finished trailers over to old man Oliver's farm and asked if he could put a few of his cows in the trailer to see if it would contain them. He put four and they had plenty of room. He added six more and still they had room to move about. He added four more and they had move-about room, but couldn't cause a shift in the trailer load. He unloaded the cows, thanked old man Oliver and took the tractor and trailer back to his shop. On Thursday, Daniel and his cousin Willie came to pick up the trailers. They were just as he had envisioned them. Nothing was going to break through those sides.

Monday morning, they picked up the herd of buffalo. Again, Daniel had underestimated the challenges of this job. There were fourteen fully grown buffalo and fourteen young. He was committed now and would just have to deal with it. He couldn't make another decision today.

The ride was smooth on the flat plains, but it was a different story when they got to the Rockies.

Both trailers crept up the mountain highway and they sighed in relief when they saw the tunnel. The climb was over. They would go through the center of the mountain and back on level ground on the other side. WRONG. The sign read, "7% grade, truckers use lower gears. Runaway truck ramps every mile."

Daniel radioed Willie, who was now shaking in his boots, that they were going to take it really slow and keep a big space between us. He started down that mountain and the buffalo shifted to the tractor end of the trailer. His speed picked up and he was flying down that mountain, trailer body swaying and buffalo bellowing their discontent. Willie was right behind him cussing all the way. Somehow, they survived the mountain ride and got back on flat pavement. They stopped for the night at Cairo, Illinois. It would be a long day tomorrow, twelve or more hours, but they were delivering those buffalo before they slept tomorrow night.

If they took Highway 55, it would be a straight shot to the coast. There were no big mountains or hills to travel. They ate a hardy breakfast at the truck stop and climbed into their cabs. It was getting dark when the crossed into Mississippi. They wouldn't be able to deliver the buffalo that night, but at least they could be in Fairhope ready to deliver them the next morning. They picked up I-10 and headed east. Traffic was light this time of night and they easily crossed Mobile. They had to exit before the tunnels and make a loop around downtown and take the causeway to the Eastern Shore. The sign said Fairhope and pointed south. They had to gear down at each traffic light which made their trip even longer. They were both getting agitated and not as alert. They didn't see the sign for County Road 104 and rode on down Greeno Road.

Willie called Daniel on the two-way radio and asked, "Are you sure they said 104? That road ahead says 48. You sure it's not 48. The sign says Fairhope one mile. Turn right and let's go that way. It can't hurt. We aren't delivering these monsters until tomorrow morning."

Daniel was tired and not sure himself anymore. He turned right and headed toward Fairhope.

He was traveling at the speed limit of 25mph when a dark mustang flew through the intersection right in front of him and two police cars with sirens blaring whizzed past. He slammed on his brake and swerved to his left to avoid hitting them. The trailer jack knifed then tipped over.

Dazed buffalo were climbing over each other to get out. Daniel and Willie jumped out of their tractors and tried shooing them back toward the trailer bed, but it was too late. They were free after three days of confinement. They saw the beds of flowers and began devouring them.

Hanging baskets swung like a pendulum in a clock as they gobbled up the succulent plants.

Daniel and Willie were screaming at the top of their lungs, but of course, in the middle of the night in downtown Fairhope there isn't a soul around. Daniel ran back to his tractor and got his cell phone and called 911.

A dispatcher came on the line, "911 emergency, how may I help you?"

Daniel said, "There are buffalo loose and running all over downtown Fairhope eating the plants and knocking down everything that isn't nailed down."

She asked, "Sir, are you drunk?"

"No, I am sober, but I want to get drunk when this is over."

"Where did you say you were calling from?"

"Fairhope, I'm at Section Street and Fairhope Avenue. Some speeder whizzed past me and then two cop cars came screaming through the intersection. I had to slam on my brakes and the tractor jack-knifed then the bed turned over."

"I'll relay your call to the authorities. Just stay calm. Someone will be there shortly."

"Lady, you need to send lots of people. Did you hear me? There are buffaloes eating up your town."

"A police car will be there shortly."

The dispatcher told the responding officer to check out a claim of buffalo roaming the streets of Fairhope. The officer was laughing when he replied, "You are joking. This guy is either drunk or crazy. Wait 'til the chief reads this report in the morning of buffalo in the streets of Fairhope."

Still laughing, the speeding police car approached the intersection still chasing the stolen Mustang. He saw the buffalo walking down the yellow line and swerved to the left and into the town clock. The police officers in the second car braked and ran into the other police car before stopping.

In disbelief, they got out of their cars. One officer checked the young man in the stolen car as the other radioed the station. "Shorty, Mike here. There are buffalo roaming downtown. Call the rodeo holding station in Robertsdale and tell them to get some people over here pronto. And Shorty, we are going to need all the people we can get to round up these buffalo."

"Mike, are you for real?"

"Look out the station door. There is one heading your way right now. Lordy Agnes, call in some off-duty officers. We need all the help we can get."

Agnes speed dialed half a dozen officers and told them they were needed downtown to round up buffalo. Larry who lives on Magnolia Street, a block off of Section Street, rolled over, sure that he must be dreaming. That is until he heard all the sirens and heard on his police radio the call for help. He grabbed his pants and pulled them over his pajama bottoms, pulled on his Fairhope police t-shirt and headed out the door. His wife, Crissie, called Agnes at the station who confirmed buffalo running all over town. Crissie called Marilyn, who called Louise, who called Angela. Within minutes half the town knew and were heading up town.

One of the police asked Daniel, "Now tell me sir, what were you doing in downtown Fairhope with two tractor loads of buffalo. Didn't you read the sign? 'No tractor trailers allowed in downtown Fairhope . I'm going to give you a citation for that."

"I was trying to find the Auburn Research Center and saw the sign for Fairhope. That center is supposed to be in Fairhope. I was driving the speed limit when that speeding car flew in front of me, and you guys were in hot pursuit. I slammed on my brakes and the trailer tipped over. and you see what a mess you caused."

Word got around quickly and people were running up the street with cameras and rakes to shoo them. The Press Register sent a reporter and photographer to capture the story. All three TV stations had crews setting up. A crew from the Auburn Research Extension Center arrived. The cattlemen from Robertsdale showed up right after that. Barriers were set up to keep the people back and the buffalo were finally loaded and carried off to the extension farm by daylight. City crews righted the benches, swept up the buffalo dung, and hosed down the streets before the shops opened. There wasn't a flower left in any planter or on any curb.

The Auburn Research Center paid the $3000.00 for the delivery. Willie was given the money to hold. Daniel spent the night in the slammer with the car thief, while Willie was interviewed by the local TV stations and quoted in the Press Register. The judge fined Daniel $300. 00 for bringing a rig into the city proper, and made him pay $ 1,500.00for the clean-up of the city.

Cost to Daniel for replanting the flowers was another $800.00. He had just enough cash left to drive home.

An after note: Auburn cancelled this contract for delivery and had the remaining buffalo shipped by rail to Robertsdale, then used their own equipment to transport them to the research farm.

Fleeting Gold

The sloshing water in the bucket held her attention until she saw the stranger. They had lived on this desolate land for nearly a year and still Buck had not found gold. Trappers had told the story of the Indian and the Spanish ghosts who could be seen in the whipping wind and the swirling snow.

Withered Grey Fox told the story he had heard from his elders that had been passed down through the generations of the Spaniards' search for the city of gold. They were dressed in armor and the natives thought they were sent by the god of the sun, so they took the Spaniards up the mountain to their sacred cave of gold. The Spaniards were greedy and wanted it all. They sent men back for supplies. The few who stayed began to dig for gold.

The elders realized their mistake. This angered the elders of the tribe. Mother Earth and the sacred mountain were being defiled. They must purge the sacred mountain of the Spanish thieves and disguise the land so no others could come and take the sun from the sacred cave.

Tall One was chosen to lead the Spaniards away. The Indian crept into the Spaniards' tent one night and signed to tell the Conquistadors of a larger cave of gold. He would lead them to it, but they must leave before his people rose from their pallets.

For three days they crisscrossed the same mountain before their decent. The canyon walls were close and seemed to smother them. The Spaniards were frightened. They stopped amid an outcropping of rocks. He showed them the cave and they were eager to go inside, but Tall One signed “Tomorrow”.

Dark clouds turned out the moon and he stole away as they slept. He climbed the mountain, for his people had moved their camp and brushed away all traces of their being there with the sweeping limbs.

During the night torrents of rain pelted the Spaniards. They were frightened. They were swept away by the flood.

More Spaniards came but could not find their men. Years passed and others were sent and returned empty-handed until they ceased coming.

People thought Grey Fox was crazy. They listened to his story, but didn't believe them. But Buck wondered.

"Honey, it will just be a year. If I don't find gold, we'll move on." Baggage in hand, they loaded their wagon and bought extra supplies. The two mules struggled to climb the rutted path until they found the trappers’ shack by the stream. They unpacked the wagon and put the wagon to the side of the shack. Buck tied the mules to the scraggly tree in the yard close enough for them to get water from the stream and eat the grass and plants nearby.

Buck left each morning and the silence began. For nine months his wife endured the daily loneliness of this place.

"Three more months," she mumbled as she carried the two buckets of water back to the shack. She felt a presence many times before, but saw nothing. that is, until today. He stood there with piercing eyes, then vanished. The sighting unnerved her. That night as they lay in bed she asked, "Do you believe in spirits?" He stiffened and asked his wife, "Why?"

"Maybe it's my imagination, but lately when I'm outside I feel eyes watching me. Today, it was a Conquistador with crazed eyes, then an Indian."

Her husband pulled her closer and said, "It's nothing, sleep, I'm with you." As he held her, he remembered the uneasy feeling he'd had as he chipped rock and searched the rock crannies for the cave. Was he close to the gold? Was this an omen?

Yesterday, he had seen the glint of gold and raced up the mountain with his battered buck and pick. He crisscrossed the ridges, but everything was unfamiliar. Confused and tired, he lay down just inside a cave entrance and slept. He tossed and turned, jerking violently as the figures appeared - the crazed-eyed Spaniard then the Tall One whose eyes penetrated his mind and told him to leave. He ran not looking back.

His wife had the same vision and packed. He pulled her into his arms, saw the packed belongings and said, "It's time to go."

Pebbles ran down before them on their journey down the mountain. Dark clouds turned to rain and the roar of the rushing water and the tingle of the single piece of metal echoed in the canyon below. Only the bucket remained as a sentinel to man's folly.

The Missing Piece

The moving van pulled away from the only home I'd ever known. My parents gave the keys to the new owner and called me to get in the car. I was next door saying goodbye to Denise, my best friend. We had lived next door to each other all of our eight years of life. We rode tricycles up and down the sidewalk as toddlers, chatted all the way to kindergarten, first and second grade, climbed the apple tree in my backyard, and built forts under the elm tree in her yard. Why did we have to move from Indiana to North Dakota? Couldn't my dad keep his job here?

Denise clung to me in our goodbye hug with tears dripping on my shoulder and my tears spattering her blouse. My mom separated us, then dragged me to the car as Denise burst out in loud cries, "Don't go. Please don't go!"

I climbed in the back seat, rolled down the window, stuck my head and half my body out the window with tears falling and waved to her until she slowly disappeared from view.

Denise and I wrote each other every week for three years after the move. She shared school, new friends, sports, and that the apple tree had died from neglect of children climbing its branches. I wrote of the cold, blizzards, frozen ponds for ice skating, hockey, and very long bus rides to school. As the years passed and high school romances blossomed, I quit writing to her.

After high school, I joined the Air Forces and was stationed in California, North Carolina, Italy, Japan, and Germany. I married and divorced twice during my thirty-year career. I had no wife, nor any children when I retired. There was something missing in both marriages, but I didn't know what.

I took a job as an aeronautical consultant and crisscrossed the United States and Europe over the next five years. It suited my restless spirit. I had a meeting scheduled today in Indianapolis, Indiana. I hadn't been in Indiana in thirty-five years, and now I was within 60 miles of Ivy Hills where my life began and where I lost my best childhood friend. I took a few days off after my meeting and drove to Ivy Hills. It hadn't changed. It was still a sleepy small town.

I went to the Chamber of Commerce to get a map and inquired if the Weatherford family still lived in Ivy Hills. The mayor overheard me and came out of her office. She didn't recognize me. She said, "I'm Denise Weatherford. May I help you?"

I said, "I'm Albert Rivers. We were best friends and next-door neighbors until my family moved."

Mayor Weatherford came around from the information desk and gave me a big hug as tears trickled down her cheeks. I'd found what was missing in my life. Denise.

How Do You Say, "I Love You?"

Love is giving unconditionally. All creatures show love and in their own way say, "I love you.

My grand dogs jump up and down when I come in the door. Scout runs around in circles and follows me everywhere, that is, after we have made a stop at the treat box. If I am busy talking to my son and daughter-in-law, Scout will begin bringing me his toys.

Crimson, another grand dog, cries at the sight of me and all one hundred plus pounds, jumps up and puts her front paws on my shoulders then licks my face. She waits for a kiss on the nose. When I am sitting or lies on the sofa, Crimson will lick my toes and lies right in front of the sofa. I don't move unless she lets me. If I give more attention to others, she will climb up into my lap.

R.J., the outside yellow lab grand dog, jumps on the fence with his head over it for a pat. His tail is wagging and his bark is his greeting. As I go in, he races around to the back deck and waits impatiently for play time. If I am standing in the driveway talking to my family, R.J. will find that hole in the fence he has created and bound out to us with his tail whipping back and forth.

Now my grand cats show their love for me differently than my grand dogs. I only see them once or twice a year.

At first, they run and hide under the kitchen table. If their momma, my youngest daughter, seems all right with my arrival, Boo will come around to observe me before he puts his paw on my leg and purrs. He won't let me hold him, but he will stay and talk to me. He will look me in the eye and converse. Baby Girl watches him before she comes around to say hello. They show their love for my daughter by curling up in her lap and allowing her to pet them. When in bed, one sleeping at her head and the other at her feet.

In love, there are always possibilities with memories no one can steal.

How I Met My Husband

I was 17 when I started college. It was the first time I had been on my own, so to speak. During the summer between high school graduation and going off to college at Jacksonville State College, as it was called 57 years ago, I met the president of the student body while he was hospitalized. He was in the hospital about 10 days and I had to stick his ear for a clotting time several times a day. During those daily vampire visits he shared what to expect. Wayne said the first week would be academic testing, orientation, assignment of advisor and ratting. Wayne explained ratting as freshmen having to do things for upper classmen. Freshmen wore red beanies with rat-like ears. Ratting lasted for two weeks.

On Monday of the second week, we would register for classes. This meant going from one person to another at tables, showing our scheduled classes and asking for a class card. Some of those seated at the registration tables had smiles and welcomed the students. They listened and answered our questions about where certain campus facilities were located, if we had to pay extra for labs, where Chatham Inn was, etc. There was one fellow, a little older than most working the tables, who grew tired of the silly freshmen questions. His body language was evident. We all registered and went on our way.

According to the information handed out about church services, Catholic mass was held in a classroom in the basement of Bibb Graves Hall. Bibb Graves was the hall where registration was held. I walked back to my dorm, put my collection of materials received and class cards on my desk and went in search of the classroom for Catholic services. Newman Club would meet there on Wednesday evenings and Sunday mass would be held there at 10:30 AM. I entered Bibb Graves Hall on the main floor and went down to the bottom floor. I expected to see a long hall with classrooms, instead I saw a construction site. The floor had been gutted. There weren't going to be classes or mass on this floor for a long time. I walked up to the second floor and looked in each room and for a sign that would tell me the new location for Catholic functions. Finding none, I went up to the third floor. The third floor was empty and the sound of my shoes echoed. I hastily went from room to room. Nothing. I descended to the second floor. The tables of registration were still up and I could see there was one person still organizing the cards. I walked toward him and paused when I realized it was the fellow who seemed annoyed with freshmen. He seemed relaxed as I approached him and had a smile. He asked how could he help me and I explained my dilemma. He said he was Catholic and he had been to mass the week before down there. He'd traveled with Father to the mission church in Piedmont the past Sunday, but he was positive there was still a room in the basement for mass. He was so sure of himself, he bet me supper.

We walked down the steps and he stopped near the bottom step as he could see equipment everywhere and hear the hollowness echo with each step. We walked the hall anyway. There was an entrance at the other end. Gray walls surrounded us, but no classrooms. He said I guess I owe you supper. We sat on the steps of that empty hall and chatted. He said he was a transfer student from the University of Texas. I was impressed, the University of Texas. Then I was curious. Why would someone go from the University of Texas to a small state school in Alabama? I could tell by his speech he was not an Alabamian. He said he was born on Long Island and his family moved to the Eastern Shore of Maryland after the big flood and his bout with pneumonia. Cost for veterans, he said, made him change schools. The University of Texas began charging out of state tuition. His roommate there told him about Jax State. I shared that I was from the Birmingham area and there were 10 members in my family. He had only one sister he said and she was 7 years older than he.

He looked at his watch, and said, "I guess I owe you supper.

"I guess you do", I replied.

We slowly walked up stairs still talking, and headed down the quadrangle to the school cafeteria unaware we were being watched by the girls in my dorm. I'd hear about it when I returned to Doggette Hall. We had the cafeteria's version of spaghetti with meat sauce. It tasted like a mixture of sausage and tomato sauce. It was more like chili over pasta. I was used to the real thing at home and kind of moved my food around the plate, but ate little. After he finished his food and watched me, he said, "If you aren't going to eat that, I'll finish it for you."

We sat and talked until they were closing down the cafeteria and Hal, a fellow who lived in the same private home he lived, said, "You have to take your romancing outside."

Romancing, we were just talking. I just met this guy. He lost a bet, we sat together for a meal. I wouldn't call that romancing, but he did have beautiful blue eyes and that reddish-brown hair is something to look at. He joked back with Hal and pulled my chair out to leave. "Good manners" I thought, that is a plus. Outside we began walking in the opposite direction of my dorm. We walked around the quadrangle and down toward the baseball field. He asked if I liked baseball and I said it was OK. I'd played softball with the kids that lived near my grandmother. We kept walking and as we did several guys called to him and said, "Taking her to the bushes?"

He just chuckled and waved them off. I thought what have I got myself into. I later learned they lived in the same house as he. We watched the team in a practice game then sat on a bench near my dorm and talked some more. He walked me to the dorm and asked me what time I went to breakfast. I shared that I usually just had coffee for breakfast and his reply was "even more of a reason for you to have breakfast with me. There is no need for good food to go to waste".

When I went in my dorm room, I had a whole group of girls crowded into my room and wanted to know why I was with that grumpy fellow from registration.

We had breakfast and supper together every night, then studied from six until nine when we'd meet again. Twelve months later I became his wife.

The Refund

When the neighbors want news to spread, they tell Marilyn. She is the neighborhood gossip and busybody. Ellis and Maxine used to sit in the yard swing every morning in their night clothes and drink a cup of coffee and enjoy the serenade of birds, that is until Marilyn let it slip that she had her binoculars pointed right at them and could read their lips. She knew everything that they shared. Today was no exception.

Ellis and Maxine had planned to take a trip with the $1,104 refund they expected. Maxine glanced at the check when it arrived yesterday and put it in the cookie jar where she hid money until she could get to the bank. Maxine started to make the coffee as Ellis pulled out the check from the cookie jar and staggered backwards. His wife dropped the can of coffee on the counter and grabbed his arm.

"Do I need to call the paramedics? Are you having a heart attack?"

He was as pale as a ghost as he handed her the check.

"What's wrong with it? Did they forget to sign it?"

He shook his head and pointed to the amount. Her eyes bulged as she read the amount: $110,400. Ellis and Maxine held onto each other and the counter as their hearts pounded like stampeding horses. Maxine was shaking so badly she couldn't scoop the coffee into the filter.

Ellis put the check back in the cookie jar and walked down to the swing alone. His wife brought the two mugs of coffee down.

Marilyn's kitchen curtain was closed. Good she wasn't up yet minding everybody's business.

Ellis said, "We have to give it back. They will realize their error sooner or later and we will be in jail, if we cash it. "

"I know, but can't we just dream for a few minutes about what we could do with $110,400? I'd have all new appliances put in the kitchen, and there would be no more cooking on one burner or defrosting the freezer every month."

"Honey, we can't keep the money, so stop fantasizing about how to spend it. I'll take the day off and we can go to the IRS office in Memphis and return the check. They can issue us a check for the right amount."

Ellis went in and called his boss. He said he had an emergency that needed his immediate attention. If he could, he'd be in the office by two o'clock.

Maxine glanced at Marilyn's kitchen widow as she got up to go in the house and start breakfast. The curtain was still closed. She started the bacon and whipped the eggs while Ellis bathed and shaved. Maxine poured herself another cup of coffee and sat at the table still dumbfounded by the error.

Ellis glanced out the living room window as he returned to the kitchen and noticed a lot of commotion at Marilyn's house. "Well Marilyn did it this time. There are several cars in front of her house and about six or eight people out there talking to her. She stuck her nose in somebody's business one time too often. Serves her right!"

They sat down and started eating their breakfast when there was a knock on the front door. "Ellis, do you think it's the IRS coming for that check?"

"Don't be silly, Maxine. He pushed back his chair and headed for the front door." He could see the legs and arms of several people through the glass panel to the left of the door. He stopped and called to Maxine, "You best put on your clothes, those people are at our door now."

"Oh no, what should I wear if I am going to jail, Ellis?"

"You aren't going to jail, Maxine."

He opened the door and several microphones were thrust in his face. "Mr. Willis, I'm a reporter with the Tunica Press. Is it true? You received a $110.400 refund from the federal government? Are you going to keep it? It was their error."

"Look this way Mr. Willis. We are live with Station TPMS in Tunica, Mississippi. Mr. and Mrs. Ellis Willis received a federal refund for more than $110,000. What was your reaction, Mr. Willis?"

"The IRS made an error. It will be taken care of today. They will issue me my correct refund."

"You have already been contacted by the IRS?"

"Not exactly. I plan to talk with them today."

"Did you make that decision before or after we told our listeners about this error?"

"My wife and I aren't trying to keep the money. Somebody made a mistake and put a couple of extra zeros when printing. Mistakes happen and can be corrected, quietly, if busybody neighbors would mind their own business. If you will follow me, I will give you a story this morning."

Ellis pushed his way through the crowd and marched to the corner with fists clenched and pounded on Marilyn's door. A meek voice could be heard through the metal door.

"Ellis, I'm not feeling well, go away."

Ellis pounded even harder as the media filmed the commotion.

Leland Mainard was watching the morning program from the police station where he worked.

He saw the anger in Ellis's face and realized Ellis was pounding on his front door. He yelled, "Get a car and turn on the lights and sirens. as he jumped across his desk and charged down the hallway. The squad car was on two wheels as it made the corner and pulled into the Mainard's driveway. Leland jumped out and ran into his basement and up the steps yelling, "Marilyn are you alright?"

Marilyn was in tears as she ran to him and said, "It's not my fault, Leland. Honestly, it is not my fault. I just called Martha and told her what Ellis and Maxine were talking about on the swing this morning and she called Cora and Cora called Leigh and Leigh's husband overheard and called the radio and TV stations. It's not my fault. You have got to believe me."

Meanwhile, the second police car arrived and cordoned off the street. Two officers got out of the patrol car, walked up the porch steps, and stood on either side of Ellis.

Maxine stayed home to guard the money and locked all the doors and pulled down all the shades. She packed an overnight case to take with her to jail. She didn't like those pink jumpsuits they made prisoners wear.

The telephone rang and she let it ring ten times before she picked it up. "Yes, this is Maxine Willis."

A man with a deep serious sounding voice said, "Mrs. Willis my name is Frank Strick. I am with the IRS."

"Oh, I've been expecting your call. Yes sir, you can come over, but Ellis, that's Mr. Willis, is over at Marilyn's house surrounded by police. I've already packed my jail bag, since I don't like those pink jump suits criminals have to wear, but I'm really not a criminal. The IRS made the mistake. I didn't cash the check. I've got it right here."

Strick shook his head and trying not to laugh said, "My partner and I will be at your house at 10:00 A. M."

Maxine asked, "Do you have those badges like they have on television? I ain't giving you the money if you don't have badges. I hope Ellis is home by then. I don't want to go to jail alone."

Frank Strick rolled his eyes back and shook his head.

Maxine looked out the living room window and saw Leland Mainard standing on the porch with Ellis. They didn't look like they were going to fight and the police officers were laughing and shaking their heads. Leland must have talked to Marilyn. He turned and walked back into the house and brought Marilyn out as Maxine peered out from the curtain. Marilyn put a box on the ground and Leland gave her the baseball bat and said something mean to her because she was crying. She tapped the box. He put his arms around her from the back and held onto the bat and slammed it down on the box. Black pieces flew out and crashed on the ground. He continued to hold her and then hit it again and again until the box was flattened.

All those newspaper people and TV people were taking pictures and talking into microphones. They had Marilyn's picture on the front page the next morning with her smashing the box that housed the binoculars she used to eavesdrop on her neighbors with the caption 'Eavesdropping Neighbor Destroys Binoculars Used for Spying'.

Martha called Marilyn first thing the next morning, but she didn't answer the phone.

Martha drove by Marilyn's house and all the window shades were down. She drove past Ellis and Maxine's house. It had the shades and curtains drawn and both their cars were gone. Martha raced home and got on the telephone. "Cora this is Martha, Ellis put a For Sale sign in their yard last night. Did they go to jail? Let me know what Becca, their next-door neighbor, has to say"

And the telephone mongers continue their daily gossip.

The Intern

Ashleigh stared at her mug of steaming coffee in front of her. "You'd think by now they'd remember I take it black!"

"What's wrong with your coffee?" Wes asked.

"Ten seconds to show time. Nine, eight, seven, six, five, four, three, two, one, you're on." said the producer.

"Good morning. I'm Ashleigh Nevins"

"And I'm Wes Gray with the early morning news."

Ashleigh with a look of disgust on her face, sets her coffee mug down, beamed a big smile and begins to speak. "There was an overnight fire that started at the sixth street warehouse. It has destroyed a whole city block and caused the evacuation of hundreds of residents in the Hillsboro neighborhood. Two fire fighters were taken to the hospital for smoke inhalation. The blaze is under investigation."

Ashleigh turns her swivel chair toward Wes and he takes the lead

"In other news, Governor Blake has declared a state of emergency for Clay County. National Guardsmen have been sent in to assist with the flooding caused by the nine inches of rain over the past 24 hours. More rain is predicted for today.

The camera fades from Wes and zooms in on Ashleigh. "And Jeb has more on the tropical storm forming in the Atlantic that will bring even more rain."

"That's right, Ashleigh. The National Weather Service has upgraded the disturbance in the Atlantic to a tropical storm with winds of fifty-three miles an hour. It is too early to predict if it will be a hurricane, though the bands are growing tighter. All indications are that it will track to the east of the United States and only be a rain maker for the east coast. That is not the news the folks in Clay County wants to hear. Locally, there is a 40 percent chance of afternoon showers for the rest of the week with temperatures in the high eighties."

The camera turns toward Wes as he introduces the traffic reporter. "And now Sergeant Malone with the morning traffic. Good morning, Bill. What is the traffic situation?"

"There are no traffic problems this morning. Fourth and Main to Seventh and Main are closed due to the fire. Buckle up and observe the speed limits, and leave the cell phone turned off until you reach your destination."

The screen shifts to a commercial and Ashleigh motions for her technical assistant to come to her.

"Yes, Ms. Nevins."

"You've been here long enough to know I take it black?'"

The signal was given that the camera would focus on the news desk and Ashleigh put on a smile and took her cue.

Lacey, her technical assistant, turned and moved off the staging area. Carole, the summer intern, asked Lacey, "Did I do something wrong?"

"It wasn't your fault. It was mine. When I told you to fix the coffee for Wes and Ashleigh, I said Wes takes two sugars and get a cup for Ashleigh, too."

"Oh no," Carole sighed, "I thought you meant both took two sugars in their coffee. I am so sorry. I'll explain the mix-up after the news goes off."

Lacey shook her head to indicate no and said ,"No, that is my job. She can get very ugly when things do not go her way."

They waited for the newscast to sign off for Ashleigh to continue her ranting. As expected, she headed toward Lacey and Carole. Lacey put up her hand to ward off Ms. Nevins' remarks.

"Ms. Nevins, this is Carole Witherspoon, the summer intern from Mississippi State College. She will be assisting me for the next eight weeks. The coffee mix-up was my fault. I asked Carole to get Wes and your coffee. I told her to put two sugars in Wes's coffee and said pour a cup for you, too. She misinterpreted my words and thought I meant your coffee should have two spoons of sugar. My apologies."

Ashleigh softened her tone. "Apology accepted." She moved to Carole and stretched out her hand. "Welcome and make sure my coffee is black tomorrow morning."

Carole turned toward Lacey as she said, "Ashleigh was an intern here once and made many mistakes at first. When she calms down, she will remember that and will be much nicer to you from here out. Smile, don't let this ruin your first day."

The bright lights were turned off and Lacey and Carole went back to the planning room.

Carole made a mental note of Ashleigh's disposition and made sure she asked Lacey for clarification before performing tasks for Ashleigh. Carole had heard from other interns that.

Ashleigh could be very influential in getting interns jobs. Coffee was always hot and black from that day on.

Part of Carole's internship was to work with her mentor and write the script for the morning newscasters. Carole was at her desk at 5 A.M. reading over the happenings for the past 24 hours.

She made a list in order of importance, then toiled over how to say it concisely.

Music played as the station logo flashed across television screens and Jeb, the morning weatherman, appeared on the television and began his morning report. "What a glorious morning. The brewing tropical storm has been downgraded to a weak tropical wave and moved further out in the Atlantic. The rain has stopped, the water is receding, and the threat of flooding is over."

Ashleigh turns from him to the camera and starts the newscast. "The sun is shining. That is a welcome relief from all the rain. In the news, there were no major problems over night. She turned toward Wes. "That's right Ashleigh, it is a wonderful day in many ways. The

Bucks beat the Woodsmen in the state baseball championship 4 to 3 with two overtimes. It was a 6- hour nerve racking game to the finish."

As the show went to a commercial, Ashleigh gave Carole and Lacey a thumbs up. The newscast continued and both commentators seem in a very good mood.

Wes asked, "Who wrote the script today? I liked the brief details and clear language. Thanks for the larger print and extra spacing between each item, Lacey."

"Wes, have you met the new intern, Carole Witherspoon? She wrote the script and made all the changes, not me."

Ashleigh overheard the comments and smiled as she left the staging area. Weeks passed and Carole continued to come in before daylight. Coffee was always brewed and on their desk a minute before the morning broadcast. Carole hoped Ashleigh would give some sign as to her approval of her work, but none came. Wes always had a smile or pat on her back, but nothing from Ashleigh. Lacey seemed pleased with her efforts, but Carole still worried. She had to have sAshleigh's approval of her work in written form as her grade to graduate from college at the end of the summer.

Ashleigh's mood had been somber the past two weeks of her internship. Carole mentally went through her daily tasks. She studied what she wrote daily to see what was there that caused Ms. Nevins to be sullen. Carole was worried. She needed a good grade and a favorable recommendation. Finally, she asked, "Lacey, is my work the reason for her bad mood? Wes seems OK with my work, but not Ashleigh."

Lacey shook her head, took Carole's hand and said, "Look honey, it is not you. She and her long-time boyfriend broke up again and every time they do, she gets crabby. You have done a great job. I've learned from you and I've been in this business for 14 years. You are getting high marks from everyone here in the studio. She isn't the only person who scores your work, we all do."

An office party was held for Carole as she finished her eight weeks. Pizza, cake and ice cream was served and everyone congratulated Carole. Ms.Nevins put out her hand to Carole,

"Carole, you have been one of the best interns I've ever worked with. Good luck in getting hired in the near future."

"Well, she won't have to worry about that. Carole, I am offering you a staff job, effective June 15th. You will have salary, health benefits and opportunities to advance to a newscaster. Think it over and be in my office at

2 P.M. with your decision." Lacey squeezed Carole's shoulder.

"Who was that man?" Carole asked.

"He is the CEO of this TV network. Say yes when you meet in his office."

Puzzled. Carole asked, "Where is his office?"

"His office is on the 9th floor. You know the private elevator on the first floor that doesn't open when someone presses the elevator button. He has a special code to open it. It goes to his office suite. He has the whole floor. I've never seen him at these parties. You really impressed him."

At 1:30 P.M., Carole checked her make-up and checked her clothing. She wished she'd worn something more professional. With shaky hands she smoothed out the wrinkles in her skirt and headed for the door. Elden, the security guard at the front desk, saw her and punched in the code for the executive elevator and with his hand motioned for Carole to enter. As the elevator door closed, she whispered, "God be with me." The elevator opened to a huge waiting room with heavy wood and leather sofas, silk drapes and a large reception desk. Her heels clicked on the dark hardwood floor then seem to sink into the beautiful, plush blue rug as she approached the receptionist.

The receptionist smiled aa Carole approached her massive teak desk and spoke, "Have a seat Ms. Witherspoon. I will let Mr. Fielding know you are here."

Carole sat down and with trembling fingers tugged at her skirt to make sure her thighs were covered, then put them in her lap and clenched her hands to stop the trembling. She bolted straight up as the door to his office opened. "You may go in Miss Witherspoon."

She told herself, smile, relax, say yes.

The Ghost of Eastern Shore Art Center

The wind howled, the trees bent and creaked as the hurricane approached the bay. The town was deserted except for the dead in the Fairhope Cemetery and they weren't leaving. Hundred-year-old live oak trees had survived previous storms, but not this one. The wind and water tugged at their roots as the old trees clawed the ground to stay upright, but to no avail. Grave markers were overturned. Rain filled the hollow spaces left by the markers. The wind stopped blowing and the rainwater was absorbed by the soil. The gaping holes remained. Trees had to be removed and homes had to be repaired before the graveyard could be returned to its city of silent citizens with righted tombstones and cleared downed trees.

The tendrils of one very old oak reached very deep into the earth. It began to wither and leave a pocket of space which its nourished root had enjoyed. As the soil dried it cracked further and it left a wooden casket exposed. Splintered wood allowed light to seep into the damaged casket of a child. The child had died too soon. She had not had an opportunity to explore her world. The raindrops had nourished her body and the water seeping into her grave awoke her spirit and she began to wiggle her toes and lift her arms. The little angel pushed on the coffin lid and it opened. She sat up and looked around. She braced herself with the sides of the casket and stood up. She grabbed a root of the oak tree that had shaded her grave for so many years and climbed to the surface. She walked around the graveyard looking at the markers with strange carvings on them. Even her own headstone had those strange markings. The child spirit searched the whole cemetery, but found no other spirits around. She went back to her home below the earth and slept until the sunlight filtered through the branches and roots warmed her face. The next morning, she rose from her wooden bed and continued to explore the grounds. She parted the hanging vines and saw a building across the road. Cautiously, she slipped through the broken window near the ground and went inside. Large boards covered with hard fabric were everywhere. They all had colors on them. She ran her hand across one picture and put it down. She picked up another, and another. She went from room to room and found even more.

One room had dirt like the dirt she had lived under for so many years. It wasn't soft and crumbly like the dirt she knew. Another room had cold metal objects on display. She twisted her head from side to side trying to understand what they were. They were smooth, not rough like the colored sheets. She tried to reach the one that looked like a head and it fell to the floor with a thud. She looked around, but there was no one there to scold her. The next room had splashes of color on tables, the floor and the walls. Blank paper was scattered everywhere. She picked up a piece and crumpled it. It made a scrunching sound. She dropped it then picked it up again and crumpled the paper again. She picked up sheet after sheet and wadded them up and laughed more and more with each. There were bottles with blue, green, yellow, red and many other colors. They were the colors she had felt on the squares of color she had found in the other room. There were long skinny sticks with pine needle ends. She ran her finger through the prickly sticks. Some had a few pieces of pine needles and were hard. Others were fluffy like the tail of a rabbit. Shadows formed as the sun went down. Her face clouded and she slipped out of the art center and crossed the street. She floated through the hole in the brick wall and into her grave.

The little ghost did this for weeks. Each day she would slip into the center through the broken glass and explore. Today was different. She heard voices. The colored blocks were picked up. The cold metal head was back on its pedestal. The hard objects of many shapes were neatly placed on shelves. They were talking about the storm as they cut chunks of the thick clay and molded it as water was added and they pumped the pedal with their feet. She stood beside the teacher as she explained the process. The teacher shivered as she moved closer. She twisted her head to see what she was doing and put her hand over the teachers. The teacher rubbed her hand to warm it. The crumpled paper was gone. The sticks with pine needles were in glass jars filled with water and each painter had an easel and a palette of different paints which they dabbed on the wooden-covered frames. She circled the room and observed each artist's strokes transform the canvas. She touched the wet paint and jumped back. She picked up a stick with a pine top and dabbed it in the yellow paint on a sheet of paper in the corner. Her eyes opened wide and her mouth flew open. She'd made a mark. She made another and another. She tried blue and green and purple. She made dots and lines, circles and squiggly lines. She spent the rest of the day dabbing paint on the sheet of paper. She rolled a sheet and took it with her. She placed it under her as she climbed into her underground bed. Each day she painted, threw clay and wandered around the gallery. She began to hang her painting on the gallery clips and would stand back and admire her creation. The staff couldn't explain the mysterious hangings. Visitors thought they were the work of local students.

She began to come in late afternoon and spend the night in the gallery. She roamed the sculpture room until everyone left then she got out her clay object, wet the clay and pulled it into a shape. She wanted an angel like she had seen in the graveyard for her grave. She made the cone shape body, made the arms to fold in front and was shaping the wings. At sunrise, she would wrap her piece in wet cheese cloth and set it in the far corner on the bottom shelf then slip away to her earthen home. Every morning when she returned to her grave, she noticed that fewer trees lay on the ground. Head stones were restored. She would have to hurry if she was going to finish her angel before they removed the tree over her grave. That next morning, she worked later and people on their way to work commented about the small angel statue that floated across the road and entered the graveyard through the hole in the brick wall.

The day came and the tree was removed from her grave site. A board was brought to repair her casket. As the man jumped into the grave to repair the damaged casket, he noticed sheets of paintings inside the box. He opened it and showed it to his boss. The art curator was asked to come over. He examined the paintings, saw the missing paint brushes and then the angel beside the marker. The curator returned the pictures and brushes to the casket and asked that the sculpted angel be placed on top of the marker. A new line was added under her name.

"Here lies an angel artist. .

The Tinker Man

"I am the tinker man

Buy my pots and pans"

The children heard the tinker's voice and charged out the door to greet him. He came every four months. He always had a piece of hard candy for the children and an assortment of objects in his wagon for the adults. He was a cheery fellow who sang his rhymes. He had taught his horse to prance when he sang rhymes.

"I have wooden toys

For girls and boys

I am the tinker man

I've clothes of blue and tan"

The children ran beside his wagon, sang with him and sometimes made new rhymes. They asked, "Mr.Tinker man what's in your wagon today?"

He delighted in their eagerness to find out. He gave each child a piece of hard candy. As they unwrapped the candy and popped in their mouths, he put his finger to his chin, looked at them with a whimsical smile then sang his rhyme.

"I have today

Goodies from the bay

Pink and gray shells

On strings that sound like bells".

The children climbed on his wagon and asked in unison, "Can we see? Can we see?"

He smiled at their eagerness to see what he had stored inside his wagon, then said, "Climb back there and look on the shelves."

He had made shelves out of limbs he'd shaved and sanded then attached to the rounded framework of his wagon. There were pots and pans, jars of marbles, jars of honey, wooden animals, and dolls made of scraps of cloth. Discarded tools he restored for use in the evening when the fireflies twinkled outside his wagon and the moon's glow lit his camp site. His philosophy was one man's trash was another man's treasure.

"I am the tinker man.

I am a handyman."

And that he was. For a hot meal and a warm bed of hay, he stayed for a day or two, mended fences, replaced a pane of glass or chopped wood. If it was a widow whose farm he'd stopped, she killed a chicken and made a pot of stew, then made him eggs in the morning and coffee, too. Each clear evening, he took out his fiddle and with that bow he made it sing as he danced around. First, the children then the adults danced until the embers of the fire died down and sleep overtook them.

He traveled from the river in the east to the north, to the west then to the south and back to the river. The tinker traveled to the north for a month, sold his wares, picked up discarded items and at night repaired them. After a month, he traveled in a different direction. When the weather was really cold, he stayed in the south with his wagon hidden under a canopy of trees. When he found thick limbs, he carved them into toys, and walking sticks. Even larger limbs and discarded wood that he found he used. From the larger pieces of wood, he created chairs and sometimes bed frames. He picked roots and berries and made tonics and creams that cured most ailments. He collected honey combs and drained the honey and put it in jars. It took him a year to complete his circuit. He sang to all the adults and children he met on his travels.

"I am the tinker man,

I am, I am

I'll fix your broken door

For a slice of ham"

Even when farmers couldn't buy anything, the farmers offered their barns of fresh hay as a soft bed and meals for a few days. He brought news wherever he traveled and carried messages to loved ones living far away.

"I am the tinker man

I sell pots and pan

I travel by horse,

Of course.

He told the widows stories of flowers he'd seen. "I was traveling down a road and saw a hill of yellow. I hitched my horse to a tree and climbed that hill. It was steeper than I thought and that yellow seemed farther away. Do you know what it was?"

Each time he told the story the widow he was visiting shook her head. He paused to build anticipation then from behind his back he handed her a bouquet of daffodil with roots for her to plant in her yard. The widows never knew what gift he'd brought. One time, he had a pouch of smooth river rocks of many hues that he shared. He loved to see them smile. It reminded him of his wife who died in childbirth and took their infant to heaven with her. He'd wandered ever since.

On pitch black nights, he told ghost stories after a meal with a family, especially if they had children.

I was traveling west

Through the wilderness

I heard it outside my wagon

I thought it was a yellow eyed cat dragon"

The family leaned toward him as he continued. "I was so scared my wagon started shaking as the crunch of leaves and snap of twigs got louder and louder. My horse was snorting and neighing, rearing up on its hind legs. Dang near broke all my eggs. The shadow on the wagon canvas made it look even larger."

He got up and hunched like a big cat. His eyes got bigger, his voice got quieter, his feet came closer, and his eyes were glaring. The whole family was on the edge of their seats. Their eyes got larger and their muscles tightened. When he had them to that level of expectation, he leaped forward and screamed like a woman. Children fell backwards off their bench. The dad leaped up and reached for his rifle and the mother rocked the chair so hard it sounded like galloping horses.

He stayed at the Welborn's place for over a month. The torrents of rain and wind made gullies all over their property. Tree roots weakened and caused them to fall to the ground. Old Mr. Welborn was too feeble to fill in the gullies and smooth the ground or cut the trees. Every day the tinker man shoveled the dirt into the gullies and every day he cut tree branches off the downed trees. After the land was leveled, he cut the trees into logs and split them. He stacked the firewood by the house. In the evening he ate with the old man and his wife then played his fiddle.

One night just before he left Mrs. Welborn asked, "Why do you always speak or sing in rhymes as you get near folks' homes?"

He told her, "The singing lets them know someone is near. The rhymes are sung to let them know who is near and they remember me. I call out my wares and they listen to see if there is anything they need or want. It gives them time to put discards out for me to take. The children always want that piece of hard candy and want a new rhyme. Sometimes they create one of their own to share with me on my next trip. He picked up his fiddle and began to play and sang.

"I am a happy man

I don't need a brass band

When I sing

Folks know I have new things.

Confusing Interpretation

When a young mother was expecting her fourth child, her almost four-year-old son asked her how the baby got into her tummy and how it would get out? She knew she had to give an honest answer, yet a simple answer. She told her son, "After mommy and daddy had been married for a while, God planted a seed of love in mommy's tummy and the baby grew until it is big enough and strong enough to come out. When you feel that kicking in my tummy, that was the baby moving around."

He was proud that he knew how babies were born. He told the four-year-old neighbor girl who came over often to play. He said, "My mommy ate a big seed and God told her she was going to have a baby. It gets bigger and bigger and kicks. I can feel it kicking when I put my hand on her tummy. That's why she looks fat."

When the little girl was called home for supper, she had his explanation of babies being born on her mind. She washed her hands and took her seat at the table. Her eyes got bigger and her tummy started churning with each dish of food that was set on the table- fried okra (lots of small seeds), meatloaf (Yea, no seeds), sliced tomatoes (many seeds and all bigger than okra seeds), mashed potatoes (no seeds, I love mashed potatoes). Then the wedges of watermelon were placed in front of her with great big black seeds. Her eyes looked like they were going to pop out of their sockets. She began squirming, and her mouth began twitching. Her mother asked if she was alright. She blurted out, "Babies come from big seeds that grow inside the tummy until the baby pops out. I ate watermelon seeds last night when you had it for dessert. Do I have a baby in my tummy?"

Her mother fainted. Her dad burst out with a roar of laughter, and her grandfather picked up a wedge of watermelon and took a big bite, black seeds and all. The little girl bolted from the table and ran into the kitchen. She made herself a peanut butter and jelly sandwich that night and every day for a whole week.

Is There Really a Santa Claus?

There comes a time in every child's life when he or she questions if there really is a Santa. My sister and I decided that there was not a Santa and we were going to prove it. On Christmas Eve all of my grandmother's children and grandchildren came to her house and then went to midnight mass together. There were many small children who would be left with an aunt and uncle while the others were at mass. Mary Ann and I decided that whoever stayed at grandma's house put the presents out while the children slept. My grandma had her home divided into a duplex. My grandma had one side and my aunt and uncle lived in the other side.

On Christmas Eve each room of the house was designated for a different family. Aunt Marie and Uncle Sam's two children got their presents in Grandma's bedroom. Aunt Pat and Uncle Roy's children got theirs in grandma's living room. My family got ours in Uncle Sam and Aunt Tina's living room. Mary Ann and I had decided we would stay awake until they returned from mass and started breakfast. We'd take turns dozing, so one was always awake. We sat straight up on the sofa and waited. We even pretended to be asleep. No noise, no toys. When were they going to bring them out? We heard the car doors slam and the commotion as everyone came in the house.

The older kids woke up the younger kids and we could hear all the excitement. Aunt Tina and Uncle Sam's living room had no toys. We could hear our older sister talking. She was opening packages. She was playing with toys. Where were ours? How did she get toys over there? One of us, and I can't remember which one of us, went to the bathroom and looked to see if we had toys in another room. There wasn't a collection of toys for Mary Ann or me. One stayed in the room as the other got food. We had to eat in the kitchen. We figured if we both went to grandma's kitchen, they would put our things out, but then we wouldn't be able to prove there wasn't a Santa Claus, so we took turns. We sat on that sofa until about 4 P.M. Christmas Day waiting and watching, but to no avail. Finally, we were both asleep at the same time. While we slept our gifts were left in the room with us.

Now the next year I tried a different approach. I hunted for gifts. I had shared my wish list. I looked in the closets, in drawers, under the bed, in the garage, in mama's two cedar chests. One day about a week before Christmas I spotted two small boxes pushed way back under my parents' dresser. Mom and Dad were working in the store. Fannie, the lady who watched over the young children of the house and did the wash was busy in the kitchen, so I went into my parent's bedroom and closed the door. I got down on my knees and tried to reach those boxes. My arm was too short. I stood on tiptoes and got a hanger out of the closet and used it to pull the two boxes forward. They were just alike except one Toni doll had blonde hair and the other had black hair. I decided I wanted the one with blonde hair. I pushed them back under the dresser and went back out of my parents' bedroom. Each day I went in and took the doll out. The first day or two, I just brushed the doll's hair with the tiny comb that came with the doll. Then I got brave and gave my doll a perm. Her hair was curly, but I thought a second perm would really make her look good. This was fun. Christmas came and the toys were under the tree. That year we each got only one toy and a new homemade outfit to wear on Christmas Day. I got my Toni doll and opened the box. There she was raggedy-looking hair and an empty perm box. Mary Ann opened her box. The black hair was still under the hair net. The perm box still had a seal on it. I looked to my parents. They looked back at me, but said nothing. I'd been caught.

They say what goes around comes around and that was certainly true with our children. They were at the stage of disbelief. We had shared this with my family. My brother Frank said don't worry, I have an idea. He rented a Santa suit. He didn't need any pading, he already had the extra tummy. After he closed his business early, he went home and put on the Santa suit, got into his red Camaro and drove across town to our house. We had left the ladder on the back patio and left the back door unlocked.

Our four children had been put to bed at their usual time of 8:30. A plate with cookies was set out and we pretended to go to bed as well. Frank came in the back gate, banged the ladder against the house and used his boot to stomp on the roof. Loudly, he complained that he could not get down the chimney. He grumbled as he took the ladder down and said he would have to go through the back door, if these children were going to get their toys. He sure hoped they were asleep because he couldn't leave a gift if anyone was awake. They were all in bed in a wink with eyes closed and ears straining to hear his every word. He left very quietly and went out the gate to the front of the house. Now three doors down lived the Williamsons. Holly, the youngest had been across the street playing with Dana and was ignoring her mother's call for her to come home. When Holly heard her mother call by her full name, she knew she had to go home. She was crossing the street from Dana's side of the street to hers when she saw my brother in a full Santa suit and a red sack. Frank stopped and called to her. "Little girl you'd better get in bed or I will just fly over your house.

Holly ran into the house, flew passed her mother and jumped in bed, shoes and all, pulled the covers up to her neck, and closed her eyes a tightly as she could. Santa Frank got into his car and headed home and threw hard candy out his car window as he passed cars with children in them.

The Memory Quilts

I told a different version of this story I wrote to tell as a storyteller. I performed it and later received a telephone call from the Mobile Bay Magazine office. They wanted me to share my story for inclusion in their May, 2012 issue. I retold my story at the entrance of the Fairhope French Quarters as they videoed then transcribed it. I was one of four Gulf Coast storytellers featured. I've made minor changes from the published version and changed the name from "Account of Miss Farrah's Quilts" to "The Memory Quilts".

I'd like to share a story with you about a person who lived in our neighborhood whom I learned to admire and appreciate. Her name was Miss Farrah. Every day you'd find Miss Farrah at the kitchen table working on the pieces of her puzzle that were colored scraps of material that she put together to create a quilt.

Miss Farrah was frail, but she could work hard, twice as hard as most people half her age. She worked on quilts every single day. She had to. You see, $368. 95Social Security check and a $178.00 school retirement check was all of her monthly income. And, you know ,that wasn't much to live on. She made do, but things are expensive and she needed something more to help her.

On her table, she pieced together material in this maze of color, the reds, the blues, the greens, and the yellows. As she reached for another piece, she saw the blue check pattern. She picked it up, put it in her hand and felt it. She remembered it. It was the blue check that she had used to make a dress to wear when her son, Calvin, graduated from high school. She remembered the smile on his face as he went across that stage. Why, it lit up her face too! She was so proud of her son.

She recalled all the arguments they'd had along the way. When he was 14, he wanted to quit school and go to work because things were so tough for him and his mom. His mama said, "No Calvin, you can't quit school. We'll make do. With tears in her eyes she said, if you have an education, you can do better. Stay in school. He silently sat there and watched as his mother picked up another scrap of material. She said, "Calvin, I value an education. No one said life was going to be easy. "

One afternoon in early fall of Calvin's junior year of high school, he again brought up the subject of his quitting school. "Momma, I'm sixteen! The law says I 'm legally able to work. Why do you insist I stay in school?"

"Calvin, we have had this conversation over and over again. The answer is NO! You can't quit school. It is the only way to a better life."

"But Momma, you let me work this summer and it has been nice to have a few dollars in my pocket and take Bette out on a real date."

"I'm glad you found summer work and you enjoyed going places with your friends, but it was a summer job when school was not in session. End of discussion, Calvin."

"Momma, you say that whenever you don't want to listen to me. It's not fair."

Miss Farrah could feel her cheeks burning as she whirled around to face her son. "I have a sixth- grade education, not because I wanted to quit school, but because I had to go to work. We were that poor. My life has been limited because of that. I don't want the same for you."

"Momma, I've heard all of this. What's the point? If I can make a living without a high school diploma, why do I need to stay in school?" Calvin paced around the kitchen his face knotted with anger. He continued in a calmer, pleading tone, "We just scrape by. We can't afford new clothes or even a TV. You have to be so tight with money."

Tears swelled in her eyes as she began to talk. "I didn't want to get up before day break and go to work in Mrs. Mallory's cafeteria. Times were very hard. I had no choice. Everybody had to work if we were to stay together as a family. Your granddaddy could hardly read or write. He had no choice, he had to work in the mines. When they were on strike, there was no money. He had to charge at the company store. After a strike, the company took what was owed out of his check before he got it. He was always in debt to the company store. Then he got lung problems and couldn't work and died that winter."

Calvin's momma broke down and cried before she could go on. "When I'd finished the sixth grade, things got really tough for my family. And if everybody in the family hadn't worked, we wouldn't have been able to stay together."

She picked up another piece of material and stitched as she talked. A tear dropped on the quilt she was making.

Calvin saw the tears slide down her cheeks and fall to the fabric in her hands. "Momma, please don't cry."

"Every morning, when the blanket of darkness was lifted and the sun of the day appeared, I dressed and I ran down that dirt road to the town square to Mrs. Mallory's boarding house. I went in the musical, squeaking back door and tied on my pink flowered apron first thing. Then I reached high on tiptoes, got down that gray earthen bowl, put in flour, shortening, baking powder, powdered milk, and water. I stirred up those biscuits, patted them out and set them in the oven. I fried up some ham and eggs and opened some of the blackberry jam I had helped make. I'd start the coffee, then set it out on the table. When the men and women came down, they always said, 'Oh, this is the best food I've ever eaten. It's better than any food within 15 miles of here. That always made me beam.

"Now, I couldn't eat anything until everyone of the boarders had finished and I'd cleaned up the whole kitchen. Then I'd take that one single biscuit that was always left, put a half slice of ham in it and a heaping spoonful of blackberry jam. This was my biggest meal of the day. As I ate, I thought about making that blackberry jam and how we'd took those berries and cooked 'em and then ladled the syrup into the jars, sealed them, cooled and put them on the shelves to use later. My pink apron was speckled with that purple berry juice. Do you now understand why it is important that you stay in school, Calvin? "

His mom looked down at that quilt she was putting together and saw she had a piece of that little pink apron. She pointed to it and said, "For you see, one bone chilling evening when I was goin' home, and it got even colder then the rain began to come ,I ran as fast as I could and my apron got caught on a piece of wire fence and tore. It was too pretty a piece of material not to keep, so I washed it and put it aside thinking someday I might find a use for it." And she had as a part of this quilt.

"Your daddy and I got married when I was 36 and you were born five years later. Your daddy got tired of the burden of us as a family and left when you were 6 years old. I worked at the school in the cafeteria until I had to retire because of my heart condition. The $178.00 school pension and the $367.95 Social Security check isn't enough, so I make ends meet by making quilts."

On the third of the month, Miss Farrah always sat by her kitchen's window. Through her lace curtains she could see the postman coming up the steps. She knew he'd have her school pension check and her Social Security check. It would be all the money for the month. It had to last her. She had the rent on the duplex, the utility bills, groceries and money for Calvin's needs.

After the postman left, she'd walk down the hill to the family-owned grocery store, pay on her grocery account then look for dented canned goods, day-old meat, and vegetables starting to wilt. Mrs. Lena, one of the owners, would say, "Miss Farrah, you don't have to buy that. Do you see that bunch of turnip greens over there?" as she pointed. "It's got a few leaves starting to turn, why don't you take them home. I've already cooked a mess of turnips for my family."

When Mrs. Lena added up the groceries, she would skip a few and then skip a few more, so that the total was never more than $10.00. Mrs. Lena would then add a few more vegetables that would go bad if not used soon in another bag and have Mr. Plumer, who worked there, drive Miss Farrah home.

Miss Farrah's neighbors understood she was having a hard time, and they understood they had to work around her pride to help her so, they'd drop by with a thick slice of meatloaf or a slice of pie they'd baked that day. They'd bring over scraps of material, a worn blanket, and ten spools of number 8 thread. They'd say, "Miss Farrah, I want you to make me a quilt with these scrap memories. I want these on my bed so every time I see the beautiful quilt, I can see the memories of my children."

Mrs. Lena was my mother. Miss Farrah made me four quilts, one for each of my children. I want to tell you about one of them. You see that red satin that is in different places on that quilt? When my aunt's cape got too old and tattered looking, she took it apart, that was the lining from

Aunt Yara's cape. The inside was red satin, and the outside was black wool. When it got too old, she took it apart, and I got the red satin.

Do you see that white, green, and yellow polka dot material? That was my little girl's jumper. She had the prettiest blue eyes and blonde curls, and she would twirl around in that jumper. She was so happy when she wore it. I'm glad I saved that piece of material. It reminds me of my little girl and the dress I had stitched for her a long time ago, one stitch at a time.

The brown and green check is a scrap from a dress I made in home economics when I was in the seventh grade. Everybody had to make a jumper. It was the first dress I had ever sewed.

I put in stitches and took out seams up and down, until finally I thought that material was going to split before I got it together.

Do you see that green, white, and gold border around the edge of the quilt? That was my grandma's kitchen curtains when I was a little girl. When she got tired of them, and made new ones, she gave the material to my mama. My mama had a new garbage can that she stored her scraps . Miss Farrah picked out those old curtains from mama's scrap can.

I love the quilts Miss Farrow made, stitched with memories and love.

Only in My Family

One spring Saturday, my husband, Ed, helped our next-door neighbor take down a greenhouse in his backyard. In the process, a support beam came loose and hit my husband in the head. He yelled, "JO, I'M HURT!"

I ran outside and Roger, a neighbor, ran across the street to help. My husband had a gash in his head and was bleeding profusely. Another neighbor, Barbara, kept our four children as Roger drove us to the hospital. Ed had a concussion and the doctor wanted him to stay at the hospital for a while. Roger and I were sitting in the waiting room when the lady at the desk registering patients called me to the telephone. It was Barbara who had my four children at her house. Barbara said,

"Jo, Kathy fell in my rock garden. She has a broken arm. I can see the bone sticking out under the skin. Roger can bring Ed home and stay with him and I'll stay with you while they set Kathy's arm.

Ed had a bandage on his head and Kathy had a cast on her arm. The following Saturday, the neighbors came over to see the injured. The children all went to the living room/tumbling room with a regulated tumbling mat instead of furniture and took turns on the mat. Dawn, our second daughter, landed wrong and fractured her wrist.

Now we had my husband with a bandage on his head and two daughters with a cast on their arms.

That same weekend our son went on a Boy Scout trip in Mississippi. On Sunday evening we met the bus at the United Methodist Church. Bill, the scout master, got off the bus and handed us our son's shattered glasses and said, "You know the city of Homewood always provides a policeman and two paramedics when scout troops travel. The boys were playing touch football and your son got knocked into a tree. The paramedics checked him and determined he has fractured three ribs, so they taped his ribs. He is sore but he will feel better in a few days.

Our son, Ed, got off the bus holding his sides. Now we have my husband with his head bandaged, two daughters with casts and a son with fractured ribs. What else could happen?

The following rainy Sunday we were running late for mass at Our Lady of Lourdes and decided to go to Saint Barnabas a few miles further away. We were in the turn lane waiting for the light to change when a car full of elderly ladies slammed into the back of our car and knocked us into the intersection. I quickly looked back at our 4 children. The youngest wasn't hurt.

The lady watched as my husband with a bandaged head, two daughters with casts on their arms, and a son holding his rib cage got out of the car.

She asked, "Did I do all that?"

Miniature Lighthouse

I was traveling in Maine when I opened the Sunday paper and found a section for unclaimed estates. I don't know why I opened it and looked for the family name, but I did, and there before me was the estate of Joseph Harrelson. It had been many years since I'd been to my grandparents retreat by the sea. I hadn't even thought of it in years. My grandparents and parents had died years ago. Surely, this could not be my grandfather. I took the number and put the section in my luggage. I had two more days of conferences in the area and then I was taking a few days of vacation. I might just as well drive up to the old estate. I don't even know if it was ever sold or if anyone lived in the weathered six room house that overlooked the water.

I was twenty-two the last summer I visited. I had just finished college and my grandfather and I sat on the cliff and watched the waves race to the shore then return to the sea. I recalled him telling me, "Always keep what is important in mind and let the other things in life take care of themselves. I've watched you grow from the small child that helped me build the wooden path and asked a thousand questions, to the young man you are today. Like your parents, I'm very proud of you."

We sat there all afternoon. The sound of the thrashing waves and the soft whistle of the wind filled our ears as the smell of salt water filled our nostrils and its stinging spray misted our skin. I wanted to spend a few days by the sea with Gramps before I had to report to basic training the next week. The Navy ROTC scholarship had allowed me to attend college. Now I had to serve my country.

I was at sea when I heard he had died. By then my parents and grandparents were living together. No mention of the summer cottage was ever made and I just assumed it had been sold. My parents traveled to the different ports of call to greet me when my ship would anchor. Sometimes Granny came with them.

"Granny is buried next to Gramps." My mother wrote, "She missed him so, and now they are together."

Retired and free of any permanent commitments, my parents sold their house and bought a thirty-five-foot RV. They were in a seniors' travel club and spent all their time traveling . I, in turn, spent twenty years in the Navy then retired and took this job as a naval consultant two years ago. Nan and I divorced five years before. I was a sailor without a home. Land travel would be a good change of pace. About twice a year I had to travel to Maine. I wore a suit now and walked along the metal pathways after work, but I never went down to the shore and ran my feet in the cold waters as I did as a child. That is until today. I put on my jeans and old sneakers and ran along the shore. I splashed water as I danced back and forth with the breaking waves. The mist hit me in the face as it had as a child. I wanted to remember those days with my grandparents. I called the state treasurer's office the next morning and inquired about the estate.

The clerk asked, "Your name sir?"

I responded, "Joseph Harrelson III"

Many questions had to be answered before I was told the estate was an abandoned piece of property at Sea Point in northern Maine.

The office worker said, "Back taxes are owed and if the property is not claimed by the end of the year, it will become the property of the state and be auctioned off for the back taxes."

I told the property clerk I would be down on Wednesday to do the paperwork and start the process to claim the land.

I inquired, "Why weren't my parents notified years ago?"

"According to our records the address we had on file for your parents was at a site where the houses were torn down and a highway was constructed."

"That is understandable."

I spent most of Wednesday filling out forms, looking at property records and calling for a hotel at or near Sea Point. I had no idea the condition of the cottage or even if I would be allowed to stay there until all the paperwork was completed and taxes paid. I filled my gas tank and bought a map of Maine then plotted my route. I'd leave at 0600 hours tomorrow. I estimated it would be a five-hour drive. I'd booked a room at Molly McPhee's Bed and Breakfast. I tried to recall if there had been such a place when I was a child. But of course, back then I was content with being with my grandparents and paid little attention to the adults or buildings around the small community.

I dropped my bag at Molly's, had a hot bowl of clam chowder and a scrod sandwich before driving up to the cottage. The road, rarely traveled, was coated with sand. A tattered snow fence could be seen in the distance. I parked the car and walked around the house. It was weathered and never painted and looked no worst after twenty more years of wind, water and salt. Curtains were drawn, so I couldn't see inside. I walked around the porch that encircled the house and spotted the lighthouse. There was a real lighthouse that's light guided ships into the harbor. I wanted one of my own.

My Gramps said, "And you will have one. "

He cut the strips of wood and nailed them together. He painted windows and put an axile in the top so I could spin it around. He had a flashlight inside that I could turn on and off. I was the keeper, of the lighthouse. Once it was built, I had to decide where we would place it. It had to be on the hill overlooking the water, so ships could see its light.

Gramps had said, "It is too small to guide ships into the harbor, but you and I will be able to see it when we are in our boat below the cliff.

Gramps dug out some sand and marked off a frame. He used long metal rods to pound deep into the sand, then poured concrete into the frame. He let it set a couple of days then put metal anchors into the concrete and bolted the lighthouse to them.

"Gramps, we need a path to lead us from the water's edge below to my lighthouse."

He smiled and took me to the lumber yard. The planks were cut to twenty-four inches. We leveled and smoothed steps for the wooden path. It took all summer, but before I left for home and another year of school the path was in place. Every day that last week we would walk to the path, then descend to Gramps' boat. I don't think we ever caught any fish, but we had fun just talking and picking out trees, birds and fish along the water's edge.

I walked down to the wooden path and sat beside my lighthouse and watched the boats below. The axile that turned the light on top of my lighthouse was rusty, but I could clean that and oil it. The flashlight was still inside, but the batteries had corroded and battery acid oozed inside the casing.

"Tomorrow I'll fix that", I said out loud.

I sat there until dusk. I dusted the seat of my pants and turned to leave . It was then that I saw the yellow glass eyes of a stuffed animal wedged between two steps of the wooden path. I reached down and pulled the disheveled creature loose and looked at it. It wasn't one of my old animals. Some other child had enjoyed my lighthouse and set and watched for the boats to come. I sat the bedraggled cat on the porch and went back down to Mrs. McPhee's. She'd waited supper for me. She was a widow in her seventies who rented rooms after her children were grown.

"It doesn't feel as lonely when there are people in the house, even if they are strangers."

I told her who I was and why I was there. I asked her, "Do you know if anybody had lived in the house in the past twenty years?"

She shook her head no and said, "Young couples have walked to the top and sat at the cliff's edge where the lighthouse is.'

I smiled and told her, "My Gramps built that for me when I was eight or nine years old. He put a flashlight inside so it would shine at night. We'd sit by the hours at night watching the stars, listening for the fog horn of boats and enjoy the musical splashes of the waves."

"Your face glowed when you talked of your Gramps. I wish I had known him too." she commented.

He smiled and nodded, "I'd like to stay an extra week If I can get the cottage cleaned up enough and get the power turned on, I'll stay there, but I doubt I can bring it back to life in just a week. Do you know of any handy man in the area who could help me with repairs?"

"Kenny Ellard fixes most everything the locals can't fix for themselves. He lives on the block behind me in the dark green house. I'll leave his number by the telephone in the hallway and you can call him, if you want."

I finished the mug of coffee and polished off the slice of cherry pie before heading up stairs. Mrs. McPhee called up to me. "Breakfast is served at 7:00 A. M. if you want to eat it hot. Good night, Mr. Harrelson.

Each morning, Mrs. McPhee had sack lunches with sandwiches and homemade cookies for both of us and a thermos of coffee. All that week, Kenny and I worked on repairing the cottage. The squeaky boards on the porch were nailed down. The flapping shingles were repaired. An electrician checked the wiring and a plumber changed out the rusty pipes. I ordered new triple pane windows that Kenny would install when they arrived. I stopped each evening at sunset and walked to the sandy spot just below the lighthouse and sat down. I leaned back and turned on the new flashlight inside the now moveable lighted dome and enjoyed its beauty.

The lights were on by the end of the week and I spent my last night in my old bedroom with its single bed and faded gray blanket . I left the keys and a check for Kenny to complete the work . I'd be back in a couple of months and I intended to move in permanently at that time. Kenny and I shook hands. I took one last walk down to the lighthouse and the wooden path. I smiled as I saw a young boy in a boat below with a man who appeared to be his grandfather. I turned and got in my car. The cloud of sand brushed away my tracks as it sped away.

The Blue Bottles

Kitty has too much time on her hands and has worn out her friends on trips to the antique malls and Saturday flea markets. Though they no longer go with her, they are the recipients of her finds . She had read about the longest yard sale in America and took off for a week to travel from Alabama to Ohio in search of something unusual to add to her collection.

In the mountains of West Virginia, she stopped and examined many objects, but was fascinated by the woman's story of the two cobalt blue bottles that were found in an old number 3 washtub full of junk. Kitty's eyes were drawn to the bright blue and she picked up the bottles.

The woman, in her 50's and dressed in bright colors, told her that the house she lived in was inhabited by spirits. Kitty didn't believe her, but was curious as to what tale she would tell.

Kitty was the only customer and the woman told her to take a seat in the lawn chair and she'd get them both a glass of cool lemonade.

After a few sips of lemonade, the woman began to speak. She had inherited this land from her great-grandfather. The house was deserted, void of paint and full of cobwebs and small creatures hiding inside. To her surprise the house was completely furnished though now white with dust. It seems her great-grandfather was quite a lady's man and squired all the available women on the mountain. He had two wives, but both died in that house and about a year after the second wife died he just left one day and never returned to the house. Rumor had it that his two wives' spirits roamed the house and bickered all the time. They would move things. The first wife's spirit would rearrange objects where she had them displayed and the spirit of the second wife would change them back. The woman said she had captured the spirits in the blue bottles and thrown them in the washtub in hopes that someone would buy the bottles.

Kitty didn't believe the story, but loved the story and the bottles. The smoke inside of the bottle intrigued her. She tossed them into her find box in the trunk of her car and traveled to Ohio. I was at her house the day she was unpacking her menagerie of finds. She shared the woman's account of the bottles and said it was just a tale to get her to buy the bottles. I was drawn to the bottles too. They had a rich blue color with a smokey quality inside. I am an artist and I had to figure out how this was accomplished. I took the bottles to my art studio above the garage and placed them on the windowsill to capture the light then went about my day. Later that week, I had a day to just paint and I went into my studio and found it in shambles. I checked the door and windows to see how the culprit had gotten in, but found that everything was locked. I began picking up the brushes, the overturned easel and pottery pieces that had been rearranged and reorganized my workspace. I didn't see the blue bottles I had left in the window. They were on their side with the metal screw caps beside them. I picked them up and screwed the caps on and placed them in the window again. I noticed the swirling haze that had been inside was gone. I thought the bottles must have accumulated a gas over time from some residue within them and the fall had allowed it to escape.

I stood at my canvas and added strokes to the land painting. I felt a cool breeze and shivered. The breeze was gone as quickly as it had arrived and I continued to paint until the sun shifted and the land had new shadows. I washed my brushes, put away my paints and closed the studio.

From the kitchen window I could see my garage and the studio above it. I thought I saw movement in the darkening window, but then it was gone. I reasoned it must have been a floater in my eye that I saw when I looked up and continued rinsing the vegetables for supper.

Saturday, I went up to the studio to paint some more . The room had a lavender smell. I had never smelled lavender up here and made a mental note to check the garden just below the window for lavender on my way out. The light contrast that I needed lasted about an hour and I stopped and took a nap on the wicker settee on the studio deck that overlooked the lake below. My husband found me there and awakened me with a kiss. At that moment from inside the studio we heard a crash. We looked at each other, then went inside to see what had fallen and why. A vase, part of a still life display I had created, had fallen to the ground and was in pieces, but how? It was the center focal point of the still life display and nothing else was disturbed.

We set a mouse trap in the studio believing this unwanted creature had gotten inside. The trap with its bit of peanut butter stayed until the peanut butter dried to a hard glob, yet small objects were still being overturned. I was puzzled but not frightened.

I had my landscape sketched, the background filled in and was working on the fine details when I noticed brush strokes that I did not recall adding. First, it was a lighter green added to the leaves, a sheen on the water and a cat slinking across the yard. I had not painted these into my landscape. It was eerie. I told my husband to put a dead bolt on the door, so our intruder would get the message that he or she was not wanted. Things continued to happen. The tie backs to the curtains were removed and the drapes hung straight. The dried flowers I had been hanging from the rafters were placed in a vase by my sink. The coffee pot with the residue of coffee was empty and the grounds were put in the trash can. Paint brushes usually in their canvas wrapping, were sitting on the worktable by my easel. The blue bottles were moved constantly from the window with the morning light to the table with the view of the lake. Some days it appeared to have a smokey quality and other days it did not.

I asked my housekeeper if she had been cleaning the studio and rearranging objects. She denied moving anything and said she only emptied the garbage, rinsed the sink and cleaned the bathroom in the studio. She said it had a creepy feeling lately and she worked as fast as she could. Was she missing something in her haste to clean? I reassured her that she did a good job of cleaning, it was just that objects in the studio had been moved and someone was adding strokes to her paintings. The cleaning lady crossed herself and said a ghost moved into your studio. A cold chill went up my spine. The blue bottle, the tale of the ghost inside, the two wives rearranging the old house in West Virginia to suit their taste. Maybe there was something to it.

I moved the blue bottles back to the window with morning light and capped them, then I saw the swirl of grey inside. The bottles shook violently in my hands. I held them tightly and took them outside to the garden on the far side of the lake. I anchored them with big stones and got the spade out of the garden shed and dug a hole in the middle of the garden surrounded by lavender. I put the bottles in the hole then covered them to the neck. The ground shook and dirt flew back at me. I spoke to the ghost. "This will be your home and you can come and go as you wish. You brought with you a lavender scent, so I have placed you in the lavender bed. Your house of blue cobalt will be slanted so dirt can cover you when your spirit has finished roaming the earth and you seek the dark covers of your graves.

Dirt flew up and the necks of the two bottles turned away from each other and dirt resettled over them. Someday when I feel the spirits are at peace with each other, I will paint the lavender garden patch with the necks of the blue bottles facing away from each other. That is if the spirits let me.

The Search for a Bride

The contract agents came from Hawaii with promises of land and wealth if the single men would work for just five years. The promises were tempting and many young men signed the contracts. Once out to sea, they found these agents had spoken out of both sides of their mouths. The food was sparse and they were not allowed to speak among themselves as they did the ship's work and men stood by with whips. The men were angry that they had been so easily deceived. As they neared land their eyes beheld a lush green land with a pleasant climate. Maybe they had misjudged these labor agents.

In silence, the Chinese were taken to the plantations and shown their grass huts with sod floors. They lay down their grass mats and waited for morning. They rose at sunrise and worked the sugar cane fields. The only sounds heard were nature's orchestra and an occasional crack of the snakeskin whip on a man's back. At dusk, they left the fields, ate the meager meals of rice, fruit and occasional piece of wild pig, then crawled into their huts with sore muscles. Years passed, but living conditions did not improve. They told themselves daily that their contract would soon end and they would be free to leave.

Near the end of their contract, the agents came with new contracts and promises of nicer housing, better work conditions and greater freedom. Some stayed uncertain of their ability to prosper on their own. Some went back to South China. Many married Hawaiians and still others sent letters home requesting a bride.

Wong Ping used his earnings to acquire land to farm. He followed his Chinese customs and wrote a letter to his friend who lived in the Chinese village of their youth and asked him to find him a suitable mate. The letter he'd written said,

"She should be strong enough to work by my side. Young enough to bear my children and good tempered to provide me with a home of peace and joy.

Li Chung shook his head when he read the note in disbelief. Was there such a woman on earth, he wondered. For months he approached the fathers in his village to no avail. His friends turned and walked away when he approached. He thought to himself, if I find a very young wife, Wong will be able to mold her into the wife of his dreams.

Wong wrote his friend on several occasions and sent the letters by ship to China. Each time he asked, "What's taking you so long? I'll be an old man by the time you find me a Chinese maiden. "Li shook his head and muttered to himself. "It would be easier to walk the Great Wall of China than it is to find you a wife. "

As autumn approached, Li Chung heard all kinds of commotion as he passed a farm. Three young women were chasing after each other and their father threw up his hands and said, "I'd pay someone to take you off my hands. You act so badly. "

Now Li Chung's ears perked up and he found himself heading straight for that farmer. He called to the farmer H He called out. "Old Gentleman, did I hear you say you'd be willing to let one of your beautiful daughters leave your farm for a prosperous life elsewhere?"

This took the Old Gentleman off-guard. He was frustrated with his daughters' behavior, but to let this stranger suggest it was another thing.

Li Chung said, "Old Gentleman ask one of your daughters to make tea and let us talk."

This stranger took the Old Gentleman's arm and led him to a nearby shady spot. He reached in his pocket and pulled out the now ragged letter from his friend Wong Ping. The Old Gentleman could not read, so Li Chung read it to him adding just a tad more to make Wong appear to be a great catch. He cleared his throat and read, "I own many acres of lush green fertile land in Hawaii planted with pineapple, sugar cane, rice and vegetables as are grown in South China. I've built a house of fine wood with a view of the sea and the mountains, but my house is empty. It needs a wife who is more beautiful than the flowers of spring, sweet enough to melt my heart to create a love that blossoms and young enough to flower with many children. I will pay her passage and give her father a dowry of money befitting such a lady. "

Now the Old Gentleman beamed. He looked back at his house and the three sullen daughters. He pondered though which one to send. His eldest did most of the work around the house since his wife died. If he sent her, he'd have to train his second daughter. No, that would never work. She was so lazy, messy and a terrible cook, but she could work fast in the fields and took a load off of him. That only left his youngest daughter of 15. When she wanted to be, she could be sweet for a few minutes and she was young. With this Wong's urging, she could become a blossom, though she was a bud with thorns right now.

"I'll send my youngest daughter, Mai Li. " the Old Gentleman finally said. "She is a bud just developing. She knows what is expected of her (while thinking, but she doesn't do it) and she is willing to wander. Yes, it will be my youngest.

Li Ping and Old Gentleman decided on a suitable dowry and Li Ping wrote Wong, so he could send the ticket, money for her father and a picture of himself for Mai Li.

Wong was thrilled until he saw the request for a picture. He was in his late 20's, but his skin was like leather from the scorching sun. She'd never agree to marry him, if she saw his picture. He searched the land near his home to find a young man with smooth skin whose picture he could send, but to no avail. All were as young as he, but just as leathery and wrinkled. Finally, he sent the only picture he had. The one on his passport that was taken seven years before.

Mai Li panicked when her father told her she was going to Hawaii to marry a fine Chinese gentleman who owned land and a beautiful house by the sea and mountains at his back door. Her older sisters protested that their father should have chosen one of them. Mai Li in her playful way began to put on airs. The sisters were again bickering and in a foul mood all the time.

Thankfully, the ship arrived and Mai Li departed full of her airs and full of fear underneath that mask. The shore grew smaller and smaller. Her fears seemed overwhelming and she wondered. "What if he doesn't like me? Would he send me back? Sometimes I can really be childish. Will he accept me as I am? He is so handsome. I know I can grow to love him and be his wife. I'll just have to try harder. "

She calmed down, but when land was sighted her anxiety reappeared. As the ship came into port her eyes searched and searched for the face in the picture. To reassure herself, she spoke out loud, "The ship is just not close enough. He's there. I know it. "

With her single piece of luggage, Mai Li walked down the gang plank as her eyes scanned the men around her. All she saw were workers unloading the ship's cargo. She thought, maybe he's just a little late. Maybe the ship wasn't due to arrive until tomorrow. Several hours passed. Fruit was loaded on the ship and it pulled away from the dock. There was no one around and the afternoon sun was sinking when she began to walk down the only dirt road that led from the pier. She had walked about five miles when she saw a man dressed in a suit coming toward her. He didn't look like the man in the picture that had been sent to China. Fear overwhelmed her and she stopped walking. She didn't know if she should run back towards the docks, or pretend she wasn't afraid and let him pass. She did not move as he came closer and closer.

Wong Ping had deliberately waited for the ship to leave before he approached her. He was equally afraid. Fearful, she would run back up the gang plank when she realized the picture was taken years ago. Wong Ping introduced himself and took her luggage. They said little as they walked to the small wooden house on the bluff. They became husband and wife the next day though it took them many months to become comfortable with each other and love to fill their hearts.

They worked as laborers in the fields of rice and pineapple each day and in their garden each evening. She planted and tended the plants to nourish them and plants of beauty, while he worked on the covered walk ways with their curving arches where they sat each evening to watch the sunset.

As the years passed their home filled with laughter of children and their house grew with more rooms and more covered arches. Their acreage grew until they were a major pineapple plantation. Now they watched as their sons helped the laborers harvest their crop and loaded it on the Dole Pineapple Factory trucks for processing.

In the dust of their lives, their evenings were filled with the laughter of grandchildren, the sound of the ocean waves and majestic beauty of the sunsets. This evening was very special for it was fifty years ago that they had wed. They laughed as they thought of their meeting on that dirt road leading from the dock- a Mischievous, young girl of 15 and a leathery Chinese farmer of 28.

Larry's Dilemma

The door of the pub was unlocked and the nightly regular came in, greeting the manager and walked over to his table. He called over his shoulder in a weary voice, "I'll be needing two pints of ale tonight. Make sure it is stout with Guinness and add a shepherd's pie, too. I've not eaten since breakfast"

The manager, sensing something was wrong, relayed the order to the cook and poured the pint of ale and a glass of coke for himself. He walked slowly to the table watching his customer to see if he could get some insight into his gloom this evening. He had his sports jacket on, his tie pulled down and his top shirt button undone. He looked older tonight, unsettled, and whipped. The age lines on his face were deep like the problem he was wrestling within his mind and soul.

Sean plopped down the drinks, but the man did not acknowledge his presence. He spoke to him and he was jolted from his thoughts and looked up with a startled look. It took him several minutes before he could focus. Sean pulled out the rickety chair and as he did, the arm came loose and he plopped it back in place with a loud popping sound. He made a mental note to remove it from the table when he got up. He asked, "Larry are you alright? Do you need an ear to listen? "

Larry just stared, then anger rose within him and he pounded his fist on the table. "I've given 23 years of my life to that paper and now they tell me they are letting me go. My ideas aren't in tune with the times. Some young kid who is still wet behind the ears is going to replace me. Replace me do you hear?"

He reached for his ale and took a long drink. He was silent and sullen and shaking his head. The giggle of the young woman who entered the pub with her friend brought him back to reality and he took another swallow.

Sean rose and seated the young couple in the far away corner so they could have some intimate time together. He brought the menus over but dropped them as he looked back at Larry and tried to place the menus on the table. He apologized to the couple, removed his towel from his back pocket and wiped off the menus. He suggested ale, but she wanted red wine and he a bottle of light beer. They said, "We will wait awhile to order food. The bottle and wine glass clinked and the young couple bubbled with soft voices and whispered sweet nothings all evening. The pub quickly filled with other regulars and a group of guys sitting at the high table watching the basketball game. The TV blared and from the table came loud boisterous yells and slaps on the back. The other waiter arrived as did the bartender and the hum of the restaurant brought a smile to the manager's face. There was the rhythmic sound of ice clicking as the bartender mixed the drinks. His arm was moving back and forth. His shoulders were moving as if music was playing. Fits of laughter and deep chuckles came from the table of six who sat by the door. They were all in their late twenties or early thirties.

Larry watched them as he ate his shepherd's pie and drank his ale. Their gaiety annoyed him, but he rationalized, they were young and hadn't learned of the heartbreak life could deal. Let them have their fun. Someday, they too would feel pain.

Again, his mind went back to the news he'd been given as he got his jacket to leave work. "Larry, we are letting you go. Your writing is stale, it isn't attracting the readers as it once had. You'll get a good severance pay and a recommendation. Next Friday is your last day."

"Stale, stale, they think my writing is stale. People aren't reading what I write!"

He unrolled the silverware from the napkin, took his pen from his pocket and set it by his plate. He looked at every person in that pub. He listened to their laughter and their loud happy cheers. He watched in wonder as the couples sat and talked, shared special looks and whispered. Between bites he scribbled on the napkin. His deep wrinkles melted away, his shoulders were no longer hunched, His mind was soaking up the atmosphere of this small place that he spent every evening drinking an ale and wolfing down a sandwich or full meal. But not tonight! Tonight, he was taking in everything, every sound, every gesture, every mood. He looked up as the silverware was dropped and bounced across the floor with a loud clinking sound. He watched as the waiters greeted the customers, took orders, exchanged pleasantries and bused tables. There was the thud of glass plates and scrapping sound as meals were placed at the serving window.

Larry was himself again. His anger had turned into determination. He wasn't going to take his dismissal sitting down. He'd show them. He raised his arm to gesture for the waiter to bring his second drink and continued furiously writing. He had opened the napkin and was now filling every inch with the life of this pub. He asked for more napkins and observed and wrote. The game ended and the guys left. Tables filled over and over with young and old, middle aged and singles, all hungry for food and friendship. The tone changed with each group. The loud laughter, and the clatter of silver on plates, the clicking of heels and the rhythmic clicking of the ice as drinks were mixed, died down, the night was winding down. Larry was becoming charged with a determination that he wasn't going to give up. He had a week. He'd write from his soul. He could change. Change was inevitable. He stuffed the stack of napkins in his inside pocket, paid his tab and walked through the heavy wooden door and listened to it slam shut. He sniffed the crisp night air, smelled the rain, looked up at the light show in the sky and heard the rumble of thunder. He turned up his jacket collar and headed home as the raindrops pelted him and splattered on the ground. His steps quickened as he hummed, "I Will Survive."

Avocado Alien

Fran looked in the mirror as she rinsed her face and paused. When had those little creases sneaked onto her face? Surely, they couldn't be wrinkles. She was too young for wrinkles. She took a face cloth and rubbed harder to see if they were creases from the way she had sleep. They didn't go away. She looked through her make-up drawer for some kind of cream that would hide them until she could determine the best way to get rid of them. She rubbed in the rejuvenating cream, added the foundation, topped it off with blush and a light dusting of face powder. The make-up blended into the creases and they were not visible. She put on her shorts and t-shirt and headed for the kitchen. Everett looked at his wife then asked, "Going somewhere this morning, hon?"

"No, why do you ask?"

"Well, I don't usually see you with make-up on first thing in the morning. Usually, you look the same as when you crawl out of bed."

"And how is that?"

"Honey, I like the way you look when you get out of bed. Fact is I like you better in bed, but I've got to get to work and don't have time for fun and games right now."

Fran was fuming by now.

He was avoiding the issue. He had noticed the wrinkles.

"Lee is here to pick me up. I'll call you at lunch time."

He grabbed his jacket, gave her a quick kiss and waved at his sleepy children as they came into the kitchen.

"Gosh Mom, you look pretty. Are you going somewhere this morning?"

"No, what will it be French toast or cereal?"

She cleaned up the kitchen and watched them catch the school bus before going back into the house for her morning chores. This was Friday. She always changed the sheets on Friday and did the laundry first thing then dusted and vacuumed before doing the ironing. She placed the ironing board in the family room and turned on the TV. It was on one of those paid advertisement stations. The title caught her attention. 'Recapture Your Youthful Beauty' She sat the iron up and turned up the volume and read the caption again. She reached for another shirt and began to press the sleeve when the lady began to talk.

"I am fifty-five years old, but people mistake me for thirty-five all the time. How do I do it? It is the all-natural avocado paste that tightens the pores, smooths out wrinkles and gives the face a natural glow. Don't go away. I'll share the secret after the commercial."

Fran grabbed a pencil and a pad and placed them at the end of the ironing board. She pressed the collar and hung the shirt up as the hostess and a male assistant appeared on the screen.

"You want beautiful skin and you can keep it for years to come with a little-known product, Avocado Whip. Used twice daily, it will tighten pores, smooth those creased places and give your face a clean healthy sheen. Everyone will turn when you walk into a room."

A young woman, probably in her twenties, but saying she is older appears on the screen. A photo of the same woman is placed over half of the TV screen. The photo showed the woman with dark circles, a blotchy complexion and crows' feet around the eyes. Fran put down the iron and went up to the screen. She pushed the rewind button and then the pause button. She stared for a few minutes then hit the resume button. The man dressed in a dark-blue suit spoke as the screen went from him to the picture of the woman.

"This is Carissa before she began using this remarkable cream and Carissa just ten days later."

Fran looked at the transformation. She unplugged the iron and sat down. The hostess went on to say, "Wash your face each morning and each evening with warm soapy water, then cleanse it with a lemon water astringent. Pat your face dry and apply a smooth coating of Avocado Whip in an upward motion. This prevents the facial tissue from breaking down and causing that sagging look. Leave the Avocado Whip on your face for twenty minutes, then rinse with cool water. Pat your face dry with a soft towel. Feel the difference. Your face will feel refreshed and will be smooth. For only $24.95 plus shipping and handling we will send you two bottles of this remarkable whip. Allow four to six weeks for delivery

Fran gasped, "Four to six weeks! My face will be as wrinkled as Grandma Moses by then."

She grabbed her purse and grocery list and headed for Wal-Mart. First, she looked in the cosmetic section to see if there was any avocado facial that she could try. She read every label.

Not a one of them had avocado in it. She decided she'd make her own. She dropped item after item into her basket. When she got to produce, she noticed avocados were on sale at two for a dollar. If she bought ten avocados, she would have enough for a ten-day supply of her own avocado whip. She bagged the avocados, flung a bag of lemons in the basket and headed for the cashier.

At home she put the perishable foods up then got out her blender. She scooped out the flesh of an avocado, cubed it and threw it in the blender and hit the puree button. It looked like baby food, English peas. You know the color. It is that sickening green. She juiced a lemon and headed for the bathroom. She removed her make-up. Washed her face in very warm soapy water then rinsed in cool water. She dipped facial wipes into the lemon juice and using upward motion cleansed her face again. It felt tighter already. She looked at the green goo and almost got sick.

"If it takes away the wrinkles, I can handle it," she said to herself. She dipped her fingers into the miracle whip and began spreading it over her face and neck. Everything was covered except her lips and eyes. She rinsed her hands, capped the avocado whip and went back into the kitchen.

She was watching her afternoon soap operas as she ironed when her seven-year-old son, Billy, ran in the back door, threw down his book bag, snatched a cookie off the plate and ran into the family room. He saw the green alien ironing and ran back out the door screaming to his bother, "Run, there is an alien in our house!" as he shot past his brother and into the path of Mr. Morley, their next-door neighbor.

About that time, Fran ran out the door after him yelling, "Billy, stop! I am not an alien from outer space intent on stealing all your puppies, daisies and warm chocolate cookies. I'm your mother!"

Trying to contain his laughter, Mr. Morley said, "Afternoon Fran"

"Afternoon, Rick"

She pulled her son away from Rick Morley and ushered her sons into the house. She poured milk for each of her sons and handed them a cookie and pointed her finger at them, "Don't you say a word to your father. "

Fran washed the green goo off her face and returned to the kitchen and began preparing dinner. The clamber of the pots told the boys it would be wise to go outside and play.

Rick was sitting on his front steps when Everett got home and called him over. He handed him a cold beer and said, "I know I should just keep my mouth shut, but I've got to tell you about this afternoon. Fran swore the boys into silence.

He slapped his knee as he burst into laughter, recovered, then told Everett of the green alien living next-door. "You might want to drink a second one before you go inside and meet that alien."

He stood up and continued to laugh as he went inside his house and left Everett on the steps with two beers.

The Last Summer Gathering at the River

Gilda drove to the grocery store eleven miles down the snaky backroad into town for the last of the snacks. Her basket was nearly full of party foods, beer and wine, when Gilda went through the checkout line.

"Looks like you are having a party," the checker commented as she scanned the wine and beer.

"Yes, my whole family is coming, all forty-one. It is a family ritual for everyone to gather at our river place for the last hurrah of summer.

The river house had been left to Lawrence and Gilda when his parents died. Lawrence was an only child. The rustic summer cabin had a back deck always lined with fishing rods, walking sticks and towels slung over the railing. Lawrence had spent many summers at the cabin splashing in the water, canoeing with his dad and hiking the trails leading into the high, wooded area with other summer folks. He wanted to keep his childhood memories and create memories with Gilda's nieces and nephews. Lawrence and Gilda had been married for eight years. They wanted children but were unable to have them. In a sense, these gatherings with the rag-a-muffin kids gave them a sense of parenting.

Lawrence had gassed up the boat, cleaned the grill and put the meat in the smoker by the time Gilda returned. "I can smell the wood smoke. When will you start the meat?" she asked.

"It is already cooking. I was just waiting for you and a cold beer on the dock before everyone arrives."

"Then unload the van and I'll get the mugs from the freezer"

"Deal" he responded as he gave her a pat on the rump and bounded down the stairs.

The smile lingered as she rearranged the fridge. She was humming to the music and dancing about the kitchen when he returned. His eyes filled with tears from laughter. Her hubby asked, "Gilda, can we cancel the party and just you and I party?"

She turned towards him with a tray of shrimp, and said with a big grin, "Later, lover boy, much later

"Spoil sport" he said.

There were bowls of snacks, fruit and raw veggies to be filled. The trays of cheese and shrimp were already in the refrigerator. Now was time for just them. They took two steps at a time as they headed down to the dock. Clinking her wine glass and his beer bottle as their laughter floated through the air. They dangled their feet in the water as they said, "Salute"

The ripple of waves from passing boats created a musical splash as it ended beneath their feet.

Hummingbirds were an orchestra of color and music as they enjoyed these moments together.

Car doors slammed. Children's voices filled the air as they charged down the steps to the boat ramp.

"Aunt Gilda, can we get in the water now? Uncle Lawrence can we water ski?"

He told them "When your cousins arrive

He yelled, jumped up, turned, then with arms out stretched he chased them. Chuckling, he shooed them back up the stairs and turned to Gilda,

"So much for our quiet moments on the pier, my love.

There were children's giggles and thunderous clamor as they scrambled back up to the deck with Uncle Lawrence in pursuit.

"Hello Judy, Wayne. These rag-a-muffins attacked me. What have you been telling them?"

"They just love you, Lawrence."

Lawrence pulled two beers out of the fridge and handed one to Wayne as Judy put the potato salad in the refrigerator.

Crystal, Wayne and Judy's four-year-old, tugged on Lawrence's leg and blurted out, "Momma got babies in her tummy"

Gilda and Lawrence both turned toward Judy and noticed the bulge under her shirt. Wayne put his arm around his wife's shoulder and smiled at her as he told them, "Triplets and in a couple of years you'll have six of our rag-a-muffins chasing you around. You know you get such joy roughhousing with all the nieces and nephews."

Gilda turned from the counter where she was unpacking the juice boxes. "When are they due?"

"January"

Judy, sensing her sister's pain at the news, went to her and took her hand and squeezed it. "Your day will come."

With two beers in hand, the fellows headed out the door.

"Triplets," Lawrence said as he shook his head.

"Don't take fertility drugs, old buddy. We only wished for one more, hopefully a boy. Could be we might have three sons."

Wayne was hobbling out the door when Lawrence noticed his bandaged foot and asked, "What did you do to your foot?"

"Stepped on a blame nail taking down that rickety green house. Your sister-in-law wants a flower bed instead. I told her to go down to Home Depot and wait for that guy from HGTV to do it for her. You should have seen the look she gave me."

Lawrence ushered him to the outdoor pool table.

"You know I'll beat you. I always do, but set them up. I want to torture you."

Lawrence laughed, "Not today, I'm going to put so much beer in you, you won't be able to see straight."

Judy took her sister away from the counter where she was arranging a dip and crackers.

"What is the matter? I saw your eyes close when Wayne said we were expecting again?"

"You seem to get pregnant so easily and even with fertility drugs, I can't conceive."

Before they could say more, they heard car doors slamming. They heard their three other siblings and their parents arrive. Gladys was the oldest sibling and was sixteen years older than Gilda, the youngest. Gilda had always looked up to her older sister whose husband was serving in the Army and had deployed to Germany. Their four boys were the oldest of the nieces and nephews and watched over their younger cousins in the water as they showed them how to do flips.

Thorny and Carol were her twin siblings. They had both married their college sweethearts during their senior year in a double wedding ceremony. Thorny and Jill were accountants and had an office in Columbus City, some fifty miles away. They waited three years before starting their family. They had four boys in four years.

Thorny always joked, "We have any, many, 'mini', and no mo."

Carol and Bud had two daughters and a newborn son. Carol, a surgical nurse, now was a stay-at-home mom. Bud traveled frequently in his job as a high-powered sales representative. Gilda took her new nephew as her sister came into the cabin. It was the first time she'd seen him.

She cradled him in her arm, pulled his blanket up and he latched onto her finger. Her heart skipped a beat. Their girls flew through the house and down to the water as they flung off the t-shirts they were wearing over their swim suits. Bud and Thorny brought up their offerings for the meal, and charged down the steps to take the cousins for a boat ride.

Evan's wife died in a traffic accident. He had a nanny to help him with his three children ages 5, 7, and 9. He brought the ice cream maker and all the fixings. Alex, Carrie, and Maddie looked to their dad to see if it was OK to go down to the river. He nodded yes and off they ran.

"Evan, Lawrence and Wayne are playing pool and Bud and Thorny are down with the children Gilda said as she took the bag of ice cream fixings from her brother.

Evan gave his sister a kiss on her cheek and said, "I'd best go down to the munchkins and help the guys."

Squeals of laughter filled the air. The yard looked like five o'clock traffic of roaming bodies of all sizes zooming in all directions.

Agnes and her brood of seven, and a few friends arrived just as Gran, Pop and Aunt Annie were getting out of the car. There were hugs and kisses and arm loads of containers exchanged as the last of the family headed up the stairs to the deck.

The new arrivals headed for the pool as Gilda, her sisters, sister-in-law, Gran and Aunt Annie sat on the lounge chairs and talked. The fathers and Pop took turns with the older kids on the jet ski and driving the boat as others water skied. All afternoon the water churned with skiers.

At dusk, the moms set the tables. Gran held her new grandson and gave orders. "Agnes, check the beans and turn off the oven. Carol, get the food out of the refrigerator and bring it out here. Gilda, don't you think it is time to call everybody to dinner?"

Gilda rang the brass bell to signal an end of the water fun. The boats were brought to shore against the protests of the munchkins and loaded on their trailers. Children changed or put on t-shirts and began to gobble the snacks while the meat was sliced. The dads beat the children fixing their plates and headed indoors.

"Where is the fire, boys?" Pop asked.

"The game starts in four minutes, get your plate Pop and watch it with us. yelled Wayne."

"Gilda is there more beer? We need something to wash away the hoarseness we're going to have. Alabama is playing Penn State called Evan."

Gilda shook her head and smiled as she pulled a twelve pack of Samuel Adams dark beer from the porch refrigerator. She wished they could have more family gatherings. The children were clearing the tables when she returned and shooting the plates into the trash can as if shooting hoops. They settled on the quilts spread on the ground as Aunt Annie got her guitar. She strummed and they all sang, mostly off key, but who cared.

The moon was high in the sky when the last car pulled out of the driveway. Lawrence got two bottles of beer and a blanket.

"Got time for a beer? There's a full moon. I've got the cold beer. And he burst into song, "I've got you, Babe"

"Just like Sonny and Cher" she sang and they both sang, "I've got you, Babe."

They lay there under the stars and he watched her. Then said, "Penny for your thoughts." She didn't hear him at first, then it registered to her that he was talking to her.

"What did you say?"

"You seem to be in another world."

He rubbed her back as she took a swallow of her beer. Tears began to drip onto her shirt and he turned her around to face him,

"What is it, honey?"

"All my siblings seem to have no trouble having children, and we can't seem to have even one. It hurts to long for children and not bear them."

More tears fell and a pained tenseness came over him as he pulled her into his arms. "We've waited eight years, maybe it's time we talk to an adoption agency."

They sat there in the moonlight and made plans for a visit to an adoption agency on Monday.

Breaking News

And now your local news with Bubba Lostbrain in our studio and Sally Seismical on location in the Afar Desert in Razophia.

"Good evening, Bubba Lostbrain reporting. Last night scientists from all nations announced that earthquakes and volcanic events have occurred in the Afar Desert during the last 3 million years. The land has a deep depression where these rifts have occurred and now it appears this is causing a new ocean to form that will rip Africa apart. FOLKS THIS IS UNBELIEVABLE! In just one million years there will be two African continents and a new ocean. This area, prone to earthquakes and volcanoes, has been avoided for centuries that is until one night after a minor fire-works display from this region, the ground in all of Razophia began to groan, heave up and down and then crack. People were running everywhere, but many couldn't out run the crack and are still running up hill to get out of the new rift. Sally is there and about to interview a runner. "

"This is Sally Seismical at the rim of the new ocean. I have with me Mr. Alda Leaper. Sir, what is it like in that big hole?"

"Gasp, gasp, gasp, are you kidding, lady?"

"No, no, you are on live TV. Share your experience."

He looked into the camera, straightened his clothes and ran his fingers through his gray grit filled hair and said," Hi Mom1, Mom 2, Mom 3, Dad, and my18 brothers and sisters. You should have seen me run. I ran down 4 meters as the earth cracked and slowly pulled apart, then I saw this water bubbling up and I knew I'd better get out of there. I ran away from that crack that went this way and that way. Finally, I came to a rock wall and I had to run uphill. I didn't want that water to catch up with me and drown me."

"Sir, you said there was water at the bottom of this chasm?"

"I don't know what a Chas__ is, but there was water in that hole."

"Here is Dr. Naeco, the lead scientist in this discovery. Dr. Naeco, what can you tell us about this incredible place? "

"Sally, we have been studying the activity of this area for centuries and have noted the changes. This recent eruption is the most significant one yet, because a tiny opening appeared last year and in the last two years 4 gallons of salty water has bubbled out. This is the beginning of a new ocean. The people of the world have never experienced such a phenomenon. If this continues to add two gallons of water a year, it will cause the cavern to fill, push the rock walls a part, and tear Africa apart. A new ocean has been born."

"Sally Sesimical reporting live from Daliaffilla-Alu Ocean in the Afar Desert of Razophia, Africa. Back to you Bubba."

"Sally, what is the English translation of the new ocean's name and when will this ocean cause Africa to split apart?"

"It will be called Daliaffilla-Alu Ocean. The English translation is daily fill a little water in oval crater ocean. We can expect this to occur in a million years. Back to you Bubba"

"Land speculators are buying up the desert and listing it on the internet as one in a million black volcanic beach ocean front properties for just one million dollars each. If you are interested in being one of the first to purchase this ocean front land, go to www://stupidisasstupiddoes. com. This is Bubba Lostbrain and Sally Seismical "Good night."

Moving Sketches

Betty Lou had always been interested in the arts. She was a member of the Art Museum and had even sat on its board many years ago. She was a socialite who wanted to be seen and photographed. As a member of a very influential family in Port Sid, she had attended the most prestigious college, traveled the world and was a member of the jet set that were always off to some exotic place or flying to New York or Chicago for dinner and a show.

After she found her husband had a mistress and wanted a divorce, she withdrew from her social outings and concentrated on a long-ago love of art. She wrote to Claire Bedford, the renowned painter and invited her to visit. She had met Ms. Bedford at several galas in New York. She had even arranged for her to have a show at the Museum of Art two years ago. She had been her house guest during that month. Betty Lou thought if she could find something to divert her attention, she could endure the humiliation of Howard's liaison. She learned many of her friends knew of his affair and had known for years. Were they really her friends? Tears trickled down her cheeks as she thought about the deception. She picked up her pen again and finished the note, tore it up and dropped her face into her hands. Her crying was so loud her housekeeper came to the door, but did not say anything. She turned and fixed a cup of hot tea and brought it into her. "I thought you might like a cup of tea. It is a bit chilly here on the sun porch. She looked up with smeared make-up cascading down her cheeks. "Thank you, Margaret".

"Can I get you anything else?"

"Just a gun. I think I'd like to kill my husband, my ex-husband. Forgive me Margaret, I really didn't mean that.

Margaret excused herself and Betty Lou picked up another piece of the embossed stationary.

She hesitated, then wrote, "Claire, my dear friend, I am in a dreadful state and need you here to console me. That bastard of a husband, pardon me, ex-husband of mind has left me for his mistress. It seems everyone has known about it for years, that is everyone except me. I can't face the snobs who now shun me for her. I need a diversion from this mess. I've always wanted to paint. I've dabbled, but have never been serious. I want to take a new road in life. The solitude of painting with someone as renowned as you is my only hope. You stayed with me a few years ago and I so loved your company. Come back for six months. You can have the guest house and one of the Mercedes for use. Margaret will be available to you as you need her. Tell me when you can come and I will send the plane to pick you up. I so want you here" She took out her check book and wrote a check for $100,000 and folded it inside the note. She closed and sealed the letter with her gold seal and sat back and finished her tea. She looked out the long slender windows and watched the ocean waves crash upon the shore below like the pain that swelled and thrashed inside of her.

She put the top down on her convertible, wrapped her hair with a scarf and drove recklessly down the winding road to town. She had the envelope beside her. She pulled over at the bluff and again began to cry. "I've never had to want for anything. Now I am paying an artist to be my friend."

An hour passed, then she pulled away and drove to the post office. She had never been in a post office. She saw the box outside and noticed people dropping envelopes into its blue mouth. She pulled in behind a silver station wagon and watched as the gray-haired man pulled the handle and dropped the mail inside. She edged up and did the same. There were so many things that ordinary people did that she had not experienced. She saw the park on the other side of the street. Mothers were pushing strollers, and children were swinging up to the sky and their happy laughter filling the air. Another thing she'd been denied. Howard did not want children. They didn't fit into the social world they'd created. How foolish she had been. Marry for the name and social status. Be self-centered. It was a lonely existence now. She pulled into a parking space and watched with envy the love and joy shared by parents and children. Her parents never had time for afternoons in the park. Nannies colored with her, played board games and chaperoned her at birthday parties, but they too kept their distance.

She smiled as she watched the park thin and decided to leave as well. Slowly, she drove up the steep road and pulled into her drive. Van, Margaret's husband, came out of the garage and took the keys from her. She went in the house with her shoulders held high and skipped up the steps. He watched in surprise, then got into the car and returned it to the garage.

He told Margaret about it that evening as they ate supper in their quarters above the garage. "Where did she go, Margaret? She was so sad when she left and I could see the agony in her face and three hours later she spoke to me by my first name. She has never done that before. I've been a fixture of the estate until today. She had a smile on her face and skipped up the steps. I like her better this way than the snob she has always been." Margaret nodded.

Margaret said, "She wrote a note and was crying then tore it up. I brought her a cup of tea and she looked up and thanked me. I watched her from the hallway. She wrote another note, sealed it and sipped her tea as she watched the ocean. I've worked for them for twenty-three years and I have never seen her so depressed.

"I don't know who she met while she was gone, but she was a different person when she returned. When she came into the house, she came looking for me and asked me to air out her art studio. She hasn't been in there in years."

It took Margaret two days to uncover the furniture, dust the furniture, and clean the windows of the studio. She pulled the easel out of the storage closet and set it by the window. She wiped the dust from the jars of paint. Betty Lou entered as she was looking out the window. She had never taken the time to see the surroundings from this room.

"Margaret, you have got my studio so clean and neat. You are a dear lady. I rarely tell you how much I appreciate you. You and your husband deserve a raise. I will tell my accountant to increase your pay.

For the next two weeks she spent her days in the studio. She left orders to not disturb her. Each day Margaret brought her lunch. She always had the same - a watercress sandwich with turkey shavings on top, a stem of grapes, and a bottle of chilled water.

Each time Margaret came into the room, the easel had been moved. Betty Lou painted the coastline, the waves as they crashed upon the shore. She painted the rugged slopes with coarse grass. She painted the light house beyond the wooded walk.

She mumbled to herself. "That is horrible. Everything is out of proportion. The blades of grass were very distinct. The walkway remained the same across the canvas. It did not narrow to give the illusion of distance and the light house looked like a child's toy. It's far too small to be a working lighthouse." She wasn't happy with her work and left them half finished. They didn't come alive on the canvas.

Maybe she could paint the scene of parents and children frolicking in the park. They were real to her. Their laughter made her happy. Since that first day, she had returned to the park four times. Each time she watched, but did not get out of her car. Today was different. She took the combs from her hair and let it fall to her shoulders as she walked through the park in her new blue jeans and cotton t-shirt she had bought at Target. Mothers said hello as she walked on the walking path. Young children waved and reached out to grab her hand as she passed. It was a good feeling. Park goers smiled and spoke. They didn't know her and yet they were friendly. Maybe she should bring her easel to the park and paint. No, that would be too cumbersome. Instead, she brought her sketch pad. There was a bench that was shaded by the branches of a weeping willow. She would be partially concealed by the long low branches that arched over and concealed her from view.

She sketched the swings, the slide, the merry-go-round. She tried to capture the faces and movement, but still it looked staged. There was no life. For several weeks she went each morning and observed, then tried to capture the scene. The children spotted her and ran to her. They parted the limbs and walked inside. Over and over again they entered and ran out. They were curious and wanted to know what she was doing. She shared her drawings and they giggled and ran off again. Close up she could see the dimples, the pug nose, the large ears and twinkle in the eyes. Maybe Claire could show her what she could not see, and capture the essence of life through these children. Claire had called and accepted her invitation. She made no mention of the check Betty Lou had sent and Betty Lou never mentioned it, either.

Claire moved into the guest house and Betty Lou and Claire had breakfast each morning at the table overlooking the pool. The patio framed with low flowering plants and the mingled fragrances of blooms was a picture in itself. Claire mentioned this one morning." I love this garden. It isn't a flat picture. It is alive with color and shapes. The shades of green, yellow and pinks of the flowering plants need to be painted. The grass is so thick. It is like a carpet. It needs to be painted."

Betty Lou responded, "I tried painting the different scenes of my grounds, but they don't come alive. I have many half-completed pictures in my studio."

"Studio! You never told me you had a studio."

"I closed it up many years ago. Margaret cleaned it and now the windows shine."

They walked up to the studio and as Betty Lou opened the door, Claire dashed through the door and picked up one of the canvases leaning against the wall. "The colors are too vivid. The size is not proportionate to the other objects. What are you trying to create?" Claire was not trying to belittle Betty Lou and Betty Lou understood. She listened then asked. "Is there any hope? "

"There is always hope, but sometimes it takes more time than people are willing to give."

That afternoon Betty Lou took Claire to the park. The mothers and their young children waved and some of the regulars jumped from their swing and ran to Betty Lou to give her a hug.

Claire commented, "This is where you need to draw, not paint. Your sketches delineate a form. You are happy here. Your art takes on life when you are a part of it. We will sketch here. I will work with you." Betty Lou hugged her friend and thanked her.

Claire said," Now we need to buy you the proper brushes. There are brushes for all kinds of leaves and brushes that smooth strokes. We will shop tomorrow."

The next day the two artists visited the art supplier. Claire was a whirlwind dropping brushes, pens, clay, paints, clothes and the special tools needed. Then Claire did something that puzzled Betty Lou. She picked up small pads and inexpensive pins.

"Why are you getting those?"

"The children at the park are so free and spontaneous. You will learn much from them."

The next morning, they loaded the car and headed to the park. Noisy little bodies followed them into the art den of the weeping willow. Pads were set on the ground and on the bench. Claire and Betty Lou focused on plants and the grounds and ignored the scattered pads.

As they worked, little hands reached for the pads and pens. Children grabbed pads from the ground under the willow tree and headed toward their mothers. Squiggly lines were drawn. Each was different and each with a different colored pen. Marks were free flowing. There were no barriers on the page. The little cherubs came and watched leaning against Claire or Betty Lou then racing back to their own pad and adding a few more lines. At precisely one o'clock, Betty Lou and Claire would close their pads, return their pens and smudge clothes to their covered containers, then took a quick stroll across a walking track. When they returned, all the sketch pads were be closed and stacked neatly. This happened day after day.

Each morning the two artists returned and opened them for the children and displayed their work on the bench and ground. The aspiring artist would watch them step onto the concrete path, then part the willow branches and sneak away with their pad.

One morning they again brought all the pads and opened them, then sat on the ground and began to sketch. The children took their places within the willow den and mimicked the artists. Their strokes were those of a young child. Every day for months the children, Betty Lou's and Claire's pens danced across the pages. The mothers also began to enter the den and got a pad to draw. Claire showed the older children how to create bunnies, butterflies and frogs. The pads filled and Claire and Betty talked of having an art class for children. They had been having informal classes at the park. More mothers came and more classes were taught.

Betty Lou spoke to the art curator about a child's display during the summer months. She showed their attempts to the museum coordinator. She commented about the influx of visitors to the museum if the children's work was displayed and the revenue it would generate for the museum if it held workshops for children. The hallway that led to the main gallery was filled with sketches and paintings. The local press was notified of the display. A photographer for the newspaper arrived and began snapping pictures as the reporter jotted down the budding artists' comments. Sunday's paper had a full-page feature story and collection of sketches and paintings. They were on the first page of the social section of the paper. Old socialites called, but Betty Lou would not answer the calls. She understood life now, and her money paid for youth activities at the museum.

Eavesdropping in the Bar

I hummed a Jimmy Buffet song "It's Five O'clock Somewhere" as I headed out of the office. "It's Five O'clock Somewhere and I'm heading for my Margaritaville.

It was Friday night and the margarita girls met every Friday night at a different bar for a few drinks and food. I'd had a grueling week and I was eager to drown the frustrations with tequila, lime and salt. I got in my convertible and felt the breeze. I was the first one to arrive and said, "I'll just go in and get a head start on the night".

I told the waitress, "I'd like that out-of-the-way table. There will be five of us."

I glanced at the menu, then hailed the waitress to my table. As she took my order, I sang, "Honey, bring me a margarita and make it big and tall".

I leaned back in my seat and let my head rest on the panel behind me. I got very still. The people behind me were up to something. My curiosity got the best of me, and I continued to eavesdrop.

"Will, I just can't, life -----for me",

I moved my head closer to the panel.

" ----gone to kn--?

I couldn't make out all the words. I turned up the volume of my hearing aid, but still couldn't make out all the words. His voice was muffled.

"It's only an------------. Who will know?"

My curiosity was in high gear. Who was that couple? No one would know what? They must be planning to spend the night together, I thought.

Anita and Pia slide in the booth. as I shushed them and pointed behind me. They leaned back and strained their ears to hear what was going on.

" Isn't there ------ ------- ?" And the voices faded" Not this t-------"

The waitress appeared and I raised my glass and held up 3 fingers. She nodded and we continued eavesdropping. All three heads were turned towards the wall when the next round of drinks appeared.

Linda and Barb stopped short of sitting down as they gazed at the three of us with our heads thrown back and our ears glued to the paneled wall. I put my finger to my lips.

Linda whispered, "What is it?"

Pia whispered, "I'm not sure. We are trying to find out. We think he is trying to get her to spend the night with him. She mumbled something, and we couldn't understand her."

More margaritas arrived . We were a little tipsy. Our hearing and our alcohol were playing tricks on our imagination. We thought he said something about murder and evidence, but each of us heard something different. They had listened for about an hour when Linda had to visit the ladies room.

She reappeared five minutes later laughing.

"What is it?" we all asked at the same time.

When she stopped laughing, she said, "They are reading a script, sometimes with their mouths full. She is that young actress on that soap opera, Love'um and Leave'um

Running Away

The tiny knock on the glass door told me it was Sharon. Sharon is my niece. For many years my brother and his family lived next door to me. I am nearly eight years older than he and my children are much older than my brother's three girls. Mary, Christy and Sharon considered me like another grandmother. They came over whenever I made pancakes. They would tell me what creature they wanted and I would drizzle the batter in the skillet in that shape.

Sharon was diagnosed with leukemia at two and had three years of chemotherapy. During that time, she became very attached to me. Her parents were more tolerant of her stubbornness and because I lived next door, they didn't mind that she ran away to Aunt Jo's.

Sharon had a clear plastic school bag that she kept with a change of clothes, just in case she ran away to my house, which was often. I'd see her walking across the yard with that frown and her bag swinging from her shoulder. She wouldn't come in until I came to the door, even though the door was unlocked. As I would open the door, she'd say,

"Call my mother and tell her I've run away."

She would wait until I had called then she'd climb the stairs and go to the guest room. It was Dawn's room until she got married. It was a pretty room with a white bookcase bed that her uncle and I bought for five dollars when we were in college and carried on our shoulders across Jacksonville to our apartment. I'd made the yellow ruffled bedspread and matching curtains when Dawn was twelve. It had a bench at the end of the bed with a cushion. Sharon would go into the room and close the door. She'd climb up on the bed, get a stack of the children books off the shelf and pretend to read. If it was a book, my girls or I had read to her often, she would memorize the story and retell it as she turned the pages.

She'd come down to the kitchen after about 10 minutes to see if her mother had come for her. When I'd say, "No, she knows you are with me

She'd smile and open the pantry door to see if there were treats. I didn't keep snacks in my pantry. I kept fresh fruit on the table instead. She'd eat a few grapes or ask me to peel an orange and eat a few sections, then ask,

"Can you make me some pancakes?"

I'd get down a bowl, the hand mixer and together we'd make pancakes. They had to be animal shape pancakes. Sometimes I made giraffes, lions, dogs, horses, fish, rhinoceros and once even a monkey. She wanted it swinging from a vine. Part of the pancake was almost black by the time I got all the parts in place. She'd eat, help me wash dishes by standing on the chair and splashing us with the soapy water. Then Evan, the imaginary elephant, would appear and we'd swing our trunks and stomp up the stairs to the yellow jungle. She'd prop herself up on the pillows after she had selected the book. The rule was that when I read to her in the bedroom, she had to close her eyes to visualize the story and be very still so she wouldn't miss anything. If her eyes opened, my mouth would not continue until eyes were closed again. Sleep overtook her every time.

During her treatments, my husband and I went up to the hospital one evening. Sharon asked if I'd make her some pancakes. We lived across the county from Children's Hospital. She wouldn't eat. She wanted animal pancakes. We found a Waffle House a few miles from the hospital. I explained Sharon's condition and asked if I could drizzle some animal shape pancakes. He said he couldn't let me behind the counter or use their griddle, but he would make some. I asked if he had raisins that we could use as eyes. He did not. He made about a dozen pancakes and gave me butter and syrup. When I asked him what I owed him, he said nothing and to come back anytime she wanted pancakes. They would be free. I was crying as I thanked him. Sharon ate one and a half and the nurses put the rest in the refrigerator for her. Just as I am crying now, as I thought about that night and wrote this story.

The Preacher's Sermon

It was another one of those visiting ministers at the Holiness Interdenominational Church in Beulah, Nebraska. Myrtle insisted that Sam go, though it was the last thing he wanted to do. He was still hung over from last night's drinking contest at the Red Lion Sports Bar. Sam and his drinking buddies met at the bar for drinks and the championship boxing match. The place was packed. It was the only place with closed circuit TV. Cliff, Paul, Barker and Sam always went drinking on fight night. Tonight ,was no different, that is until Dan challenged the crowd to see who could out drink him. Now Dan was a bragger. He thought he could do everything better than anyone else. So far, he had proved he was the biggest loud mouth, smelled the worse, and could bench press more weight than anyone there. Eight guys lined up at the bar. They would drink their way through the championship fight. They would down as many beers as possible between rounds. The bar keeper held the bets and the drinking began amid shouts of encouragement. Al drank 14 and had to go puke. Melford wobbled so on the bar stool after 15 that they disqualified him. Barker downed 19 by round six and was ahead of the others that is until his face slammed into the bar counter and he was out for the count. Sam was going strong by then and sure he was going to win. He was downing at least two beers between each round. The more he drank the happier he got. Westley and Buck gave up after 20 beers. They were as green as the beer bottles in their hands. Charlie was drinking his twenty-second beer. With each swallow his stomach ballooned out a little more. His shirt button popped off and hit the waitress right between the eyes. He blubbered, "I'm sorry, sweetie" and ran for the john. That left Dan and Sam. Though sopping drunk, they were not going to forfeit to the other. They would drink until the match was over and count the bottles. Round nine found them both on bottle 29. Blurry eyed, they reached for another beer. Dan missed the bottle and it crashed onto the counter. He put his face in the puddle of beer and accepted defeat. Sam had just taken one swig out of bottle 30.

Cliff grabbed Sam shoulders, Paul grabbed a leg and Barker, now partially recovered after a little up chucking, grabbed Sam's other leg. The bar door was opened for them and Sam was dumped into the bed of Cliff's truck. His beer belly made him look nine months' pregnant. As they turned the corner to Sam's neighborhood, they turned out the lights and backed into his carport. He didn't even move as they slid him out of the truck bed and stood him up. Paul turned on the outside hose and Barker sprayed him with water. He came to arms flailing, then puked on the driveway. They opened his kitchen door and pushed him through it. He stumbled toward the bedroom as they hosed down the driveway and left.

He relieved himself, left his pants on the bathroom floor and weaved toward the bed. He flopped face down on top of the covers and was snoring by the time Myrtle raised up to see him there. She shook him, “Stop snoring!”

He made a grunting sound and was out again. He wasn’t ready to get up when Myrtle rolled over and shook him. He looked at her with her silk panties on her head and just cried like a baby. “We must have had a hell of a good time last night and I can’t even remember it.”

Discussed with her husband’s drunkenness, she said, “Now it is time to repent. Get your drunken body out of this bed and into the shower. You smell like a brewery. She pushed him into the shower and turned on the cold water. He let out a howl and adjusted the water as he remarked, “That woman can be so cruel at times.”

Myrtle was dressed for church by the time he got downstairs. She handed him a glass of tomato juice and said, “Drink it.”

She sat down with a cup of coffee and pushed a strong cup of black coffee in front of Sam. Myrtle looked at her watch and put her coffee cup in the sink. She got her purse and the car keys and pointed at the door to the garage, shook her head as she stood before Sam and pointed her finger at him, “If there was ever a day you needed to be in church, it is today. You need to repent and change your ways, Sam Neely.”

They didn’t speak as Myrtle drove. Brother Louis, the pastor was the greeter this morning.

“Morning, Myrtle, Sam. You won’t be disappointed with this morning sermon. Rev. Stouffer is going to talk about life and the direction we take. Get you a seat near the front. It is going to be a powerful sermon."

The Rev. Stouffer came onto the altar in his blue robe and just stood for a minute. He looked at the congregation. He saw Myrtle nudge Sam as he began to nod. He thought, 'I'll need to raise my voice to keep this crowd attentive.'

Mrs. Cockrell played the entrance hymn as he stood on the altar and raised his voice with that of the congregation. He pranced back and forth as they all sang. With the last note, he stepped forward and looked at the seated congregation for over a minute without saying a word. He raised the microphone he was holding to his face and in a booming voice began to speak.

"Vaclev Havel said, and I quote, "The very sense of life, the meaning of life, is closely related with hope." He walked back and forth across the altar. His voice got louder as he looked at the dozing Sam. "Life without hope of God's graces to help you, is not life. You must believe. You must strive for a quality life with God at the center."

His storm of words seemed to come up out of nowhere. The louder he got the more fired up the congregation got. After each comment they shouted "Amen.",

The congregation and Rev. Stouffer were at a feverish pitch when Sam let out a tremendous rumbling snore that pinged off the walls and echoed throughout the sanctuary. There were gasps and squeals as the congregation thought God had spoken to them. Total silence fell on the church until Sam let out another gurgling snore and saliva bubbled out of his mouth. Myrtle was mortified. She kicked Sam in the shins and yanked him to his feet. The preacher came down among the congregation and continued his sermon as Sam and Myrtle with heads down left the church.

Rev. Stouffer walked slowly down the aisle looking at the men and pointing at some as he continued preaching. "You need to re-evaluate your lives and give yourself to the Lord. Change your ways. Repent. Revive. You will rejoice in the Lord. The circumstances of our lives cannot be controlled, but the choices we make when faced with these can be changed. Look into your souls. How can you better serve the Lord? You can adjust and you can change. I will close with a single sentence but such a powerful sentence. 'We can't control the winds of our life but we can adjust our sails. 'Amen.

I'm Waiting

I had so many things to do for the party I was having at my home that evening and my list kept growing. I shook my head, grabbed my list, and kissed my husband goodbye as he went to his men's meeting. My back grumbled a bit as I eased into the car and drove out of the driveway and headed downtown. I was still recovering from a back injury and I had physical therapy at 8 o'clock that morning. By nine, I was starved and stopped at McDonald's for a sausage biscuit and seniors' coffee. I didn't have time to go inside, I picked up my order at the drive-thru window and unwrapped the biscuit as I drove, with the sunroof open, to Winn Dixie. I had eaten half of my biscuit by the time I got to the grocery store and left the half-eaten biscuit on the seat as I got out of the car. I had completely forgotten the open sunroof.

I ran into several friends shopping in the store and we chatted for a few minutes. I must have been in the store at least an hour before I realized how late it was getting. I put everything in the trunk except the bunch of flowers I'd bought for the dining room table. I hopped into the car, put the flowers on the front seat, turned on the engine and put the car in reverse. Suddenly, I saw this object raise up from the back seat. It took me a second to realize it was a seagull. As I turned and ducked away, I thought,

"He must have come in through the sunroof.

My foot came off the pedal and since the car was in reverse, I swerved backing out and I hit the white Escalade parked next to me. If that wasn't enough, I managed to back out far enough to hit the car coming down the lane behind me. I slammed on the brakes and jumped out of the car. I left my door open and ran around to open the other door hoping the bird would fly away, while the other driver, a stunned little man, watched in disbelief. He was driving a vintage 1957 Chevy. And I have to say it was a beauty. He came to his senses and yelled,

"You just hit my antique car. Do you have any idea how much it will cost to repair it?"

I shook my head and sputtered, "I'm not a mechanic.

Very upset with a sea gull inside my car and a damaged Escalade beside me, I walked over to see the damage to his car. The only damage I could see was a few places with paint scrapes and they didn't look new.

"Your trophy car is made of steel, mine's plastic.

He snorted, "You got that right.

I ran back to my car and began shooing the bird with the bunch of flowers. By now the older man was doubled over in laughter. I hit the seagull with the flowers and it began to flutter. It hit the roof of the car, then the windshield and finally, the startled bird realized it could escape through the open doors. Off he flew with a piece of my sausage biscuit in his beak, not willing to lose a breakfast.

The old man called the cops and you should have seen the police officer's face when I tried to explain what happened. The old man was still laughing, and I was still stressed out. I'd just hit two cars, beaten my bouquet of flowers to petals and broken stems. The officer was trying to keep a straight face when he asked me,

"So, you hit two cars and tried to assault a helpless seagull, ma'am?"

Even I could see the humor in that. On-lookers coming out of the store surrounded us to find out what was so funny about the wreck, but they didn't know about the suburban housewife with a thing against seagulls.

"You're as bad as he is, officer. Stop laughing at me.

"I can't, you are so funny… beating a poor hungry bird with flowers. Go on, I can't wait to hear the rest of the story.

I huffed then continued as the manager of Winn Dixie came out to see what was causing all the commotion. I asked him to announce for the owner of a white 2007 Escalade parked near the front of the store to come to the service department. Mary Lou, one of the friends I'd talked to in the store, was about to push her buggy out the door when she heard the announcement. The manager told her of the accident and damage to her vehicle as he pushed her grocery cart out to the scene.

Lou, as she is sometimes called, started laughing and between fits of laughter said,

"Dinner had better be good tonight. Have you already gotten into the wine?"

Ed was home and came out to help me take in the groceries. He hadn't noticed the damage to the right panel of the car, but saw the dent in the rear bumper. Like the others, he was laughing too as I retold the story.

"Stop laughing at me. I've had a very traumatic morning."

I was crying and laughing at the same time. He grabbed me into his arms and just stood there laughing.

"Honey, I don't think we'll have to worry about conversation tonight at our party. You'd better get started cooking 'Bird Woman'. Shall I put these flowers in a vase?"

That's when I started chasing him around the house with the battered flowers and he continued his roar of laughter.

That's Hog-Wash My Darling

The O Leary's lived on the ridge with a wrought iron fence because of his wife's fears. If he walked under the ladder, she'd yell, "Melvin, don't test your luck!"

Laughing, he'd reply," Tis you that is superstitious my darling.

She'd cross herself and let out her breath when he passed under it. Sometimes he'd do it to aggravate her. Mice got in the chicken feed and he decided to buy a cat. She didn't like that idea. Cats could be bad luck, especially black cats.

"Make it a white kitten. his wife said."

"I'll see if Thomas has a white one, but if he doesn't, I'll get a tabby or a black kitten."

"Melvin O'Leary, you will be the death of me."

"Not I, my darling. "

He had a box in his arms when she looked out the window. She peered in the box and saw three kittens.

"My darling, I couldn't separate them. There's a white kitten for you , a tabby for me and a black kitten to scare away the mice."

She pulled back her hand and fear streaked across her face. " You must take the black one back. It's bad luck. The mice will eat up all the grain and overrun my garden if you keep the black one." Her eyes were as big as saucers and swelled with tears, and her hands trembled.

"Calm down, my darling, that is hog wash. Your silly superstitions are getting the best of you. I saw you last night throw the salt over your shoulder and this morning when you brought me coffee and walked under the ladder, you screamed then backed out mumbling some rhyme. "

He handed her the white and tabby kittens and took the black one back. The kittens grew. The tabby ate mice and the white kitten ate table scrapes. From the yard swing she'd watch them playing. She saw the black movement in the tall grass as it squeezed through the fence toward her. She screamed for Melvin. She saw him running, saw the scythe fly into the air and sever his arm. She jumped off the swing and ran to him as he lay in a pool of blood. The black demon disappeared.

He died the next morning. The neighbors dug a grave in a corner of the yard by the iron fence. The preacher said a few words as the black cat hissed outside the fence as dirt was shoveled over Melvin. She stayed in the house, fearing the black cat would return.

There was a full moon that Halloween as several boys tried to scare her. They tied ropes to the swing and pulled them for movement. Another pulled the gate with its grating sound. They saw the glint of the shot gun and heard the shot. They ran. Next morning, the town buzzed of news that the old lady had killed the black cat.

Christmas Surprise

It is rare that all four of our children and their families are together for Christmastime, but Christmas 2006, the whole Graven clan shared Christmas Eve with a special meal and opening of presents. Christmas Day is always a celebration of nine of the ten living La Russa/Shahid siblings and their families at my brother's house. Christmas Eve is a gathering of just our children and grandchildren.

We gathered in the family room at our son, Ed and his wife, Priscilla's home. The tree reached the ceiling and a fourth of the room was covered with presents of all sizes. Several of the grandchildren called out names and passed the gifts. This went on for nearly an hour. Everyone's name was called out except my husband, Ed, and mine. We looked at each other and wondered what they had bought us. They had given us a group gift on two other occasions, a microwave in the early 1980s because their parents didn't have one, and they gave us cell phones and paid the bill for a year's service in the 90's. What did they think we needed now?

The last packages under the tree were the gifts Ed and I had bought for each other. There was one flat package with all four of our children's names on it. There was a hush in the room, when they told us we had to open it together. All eyes were on us. The paper was ripped off. There was a blue multi-pocketed folder inside. Ed was holding it with a puzzled look on his face as he turned toward me.

"Open the folder, Dad", one of our kids yelled.

Ed pulled out the thick packet, glanced then grabbed me and began dancing around with a gusto of laughter that had everyone laughing. I was still unaware of its contents, but enjoying his laughter and our dancing.

"You two are always chasing the hot air balloons and you've talked about going to the Balloon Festival in Albuquerque. We just thought we'd help your wish come true.

We looked through the pages. We couldn't believe our eyes. They had plane reservations, a rental car with a GPS, executive suite at the Marriott, tickets to the balloon festival for all five days, and spending money to enjoy on the trip.

"Baby, we have hit the jackpot," he said, turned and gave me a kiss, then turned to our children and grandchildren and said, "Thank you. Your mother and I have been truly blessed to have all of you. With that mischievous twinkle in his eyes he added, "though there were times that we wondered. "

October 2007, finally came and we packed our bags and headed west. Our plane landed at Gate 2 in Denver forty minutes before our connecting flight was to leave at Gate 82. With wheeled carry-on bags we ran (yes, I could run) weaving between passengers. We could see the gate. They weren't loading yet. We stopped and hunched over with hands on knees to catch our breath. Ed looked at me and winked as he quipped, "Baby, we still got it in us."

Still huffing, we ambled to the gate. We marveled at the beauty of the Rocky Mountains from the plane and wondered what adventure awaited us.

We picked up the rental car and the representative explained how to use the GPS, then connected and program our first destination, the hotel. We could see the hotel just ahead of us on the left. The hotel was one block away.

"Wrong turn, recalculating, turn around, wrong turn. The automated voice repeated. He turned left and went right into the Marriott Hotel entrance. The GPS was a nuisance. It happened several more times during the next few days and Ed finally said, "Take that damn thing and put it in the glove compartment. "

The executive suite was on an upper floor with a view of the mountains and spectacular sunsets. As an added plus, there was an executive lounge a few doors down, complete with food and drinks, and an upscale atmosphere. The servers in the lounge area were accommodating in providing Ed with gluten-free foods.

The concierge said, "The first bus to the festival leaves at 4:30A.M. You can drive or walk to the pick-up point at the mall parking lot three blocks over. There will be coffee, sweet rolls and donuts in the bar area by 4 A.M.

The alarm was going off the next morning as Ed returned to the room with coffee and food. "Baby, get your clothes on. There is a crowd leaving for the buses already." It was very chilly as we left for the mall. We drove, expecting to see just a few people in line at that hour of the morning. As we stood in the line that snaked back and forth on the mall parking lot, I asked, "What time is it?" Ed grinned as the man behind us said, "3:58.

We sat at a picnic table close to the balloon area and talked with the crews, then we watched the sun rise as hundreds of balloons filled the sky. We were there every morning and spent our afternoons visiting the Indian museum, driving to the Acoma Indian Reservation for a tour, and seeing the Rio Grande River, though at the time, it was more like a gully.

The last few days we headed to Santa Fe. We had day passes in our gift packet and toured the sights. Two sights stood out, the staircase that had no nails or support in the little chapel with hundreds of wind chimes in the garden beside it. Ed and I ended our evening with mass in the church connected to the chapel.

The Native American Center in Santa Fe had a totally different character to it than the Acoma area. The grounds were beautiful with the rich high desert flowers. The history within the walls was almost too much to absorb. Ed and I, having walked the fields of Alabama in search of Indian artifacts, marveled at the quality of artifacts housed there. The native dancers entertained us as we sipped on diet cokes in the afternoon. The sky changed from a rich blue to hues of orange, red and purple against the mountains. We'd hoped to travel part of the way to Taos on the rugged road that ran beside the Rio Grande. There were black clouds overhead as we pulled into the rest area. The attendant at the rest area told us, "Sometimes these thunderstorms are gully washers. I would not advise taking the road that runs beside the dry bed of the Rio Grande River. The dry riverbeds quickly fill and flood as the water rushes downstream during a thunderstorm.

We spent two days in Taos. We'd seen signs along the road of a Wool Festival that day in Taos. Being a city girl, I expected to see a huge area brimming with people and activities, instead there was a small crowd of families milling around. Most, I believe, were locals sharing their wares in the single row of vendors' tents. Around the park were stations for shearing sheep, cleaning wool and spinning the yarn. Yarn dying and knitting were demonstrated. Most of the artisans were in costume. Very old and new technological tools were demonstrated. We purchased a few Christmas gifts before we sought warmth from the chilling rain in a restaurant/bar. It had low lighting, rustic tables, and raw bone men shooting pool in one corner with a line of empty beer bottles on the table. A fellow in tooled boots, western hat, and worn jeans sat on a stool with his battered guitar and played requests for money. Ed fed the tip jar several times and we sang along.

We'd planned to go to Durango, Colorado the next day, but the rain had a heavy feeling like sleet, and we headed south back to Albuquerque. There were winding roads, some paved and some dirt that Ed could not resist and we saw a different side of New Mexico.

Our last night, we took the tram up the mountain. We had hoped to be on top of the mountain at sunset, but several hundred other people had the same idea. The sky was dark, the wind was whipping and the air was very cold when we stepped off the tram. Our original plan had been to have a romantic dinner in the open bar area at the top of the mountain, but it was too cold for even the help that night. Our romance was shivering together in the moonlight and sharing a few kisses with quivering lips from the shivers as we waited for the tram to return and take us back down the mountain.

Our plane touched down in Pensacola minus our luggage. Sometime during the night our bags were left by the front door as we slept in our own bed.

We had a hell of a lot of fun and our children made sure it cost us nothing, but provided a trip with memories to last a lifetime.

The Prediction

The telephone rang at city desk of Metro News.

"Clayton, this is Dean Lathersole. I have been studying the hairs on the black and yellow wooly worm and I have determined it is losing all its hair. This has never happened before. I analyzed each hair and there is nothing wrong with any of them. I checked in my zoology books and found this can only occur when there is to be a dramatic event on earth. "

"What dramatic event do you predict this time?"

"The big one is coming.

"Big what?"

"The end of the earth.

"Dean, you have predicted some really wild happenings in the past and some have happened and most have not. I thought you checked the fur depth of the black and yellow woolly worm to predict whether it would be a mild or severe winter. Now you are saying you can predict the end of the world because these bugs have lost their hair."

"Clayton, the process has begun. In the Bible it says there will be floods and fire. The earth would tremble and the earth will split".

"Now Dean your interpretation of the Bible and what it really says is not the same. You are just using this to get your name in the paper again."

"No, it is true. Look around. There is flooding in all parts of the world. It is the worst flooding to occur in more than fifty years. There have been more tornadoes all over the US. People are dying, one right after another. Half of Arizona is on fire. Texas is the same. Preacher Belcher stated this in his sermon on Sunday. There will be false prophets, floods, storms and fire just before the end of the world."

"You have got to be kidding.

"There is an explanation. Now hear me out."

"I'm listening."

"Look around you, what do you see? "

"Nothing unusual."

"Look again, son. The earth is drying up. The plants are parched. The heat from the sun started those fires. Only God can make that happen. The violent weather isn't a freak happening. It is the Almighty who created the horrific weather. He has tried to warn His children to change their ways of destruction, repent and live by His words."

"Dean, that is not possible,"

"Preacher Belcher said he had a dream and the angels came with a message to all."

The angel said, "The earth is going to tremble as it cracks open at New Madrid Fault. The earthquake will be so powerful, it will destroy everything from the Rocky Mountains to the Atlantic Ocean creating a massive tsunami that will flood all of Europe. Within two days the earth will groan in Russia, Chile, and Africa. The rift will split open the earth and molten rock will cover the earth. The plates of the Ring of Fire will push apart then move back again spewing fire from all the active volcanoes. Volcanic ash will blacken the sky. People will cough then drop like flies as their lungs fill with the sulfuric ash. Life on earth will end on May 21st."

"What can be done?"

"Nothing"

Clayton wrote the article quoting Dean's prediction. People took mini vacations , ate the foods that would raise their cholesterol, drank, too much wine and danced in the streets. There was a run on facial masks and hazardous clothing. People skipped work. Money ear-marked for bills was taken out of their accounts to buy all that they desired. They reasoned that they would get to enjoy these pleasures for at least a week. On May 21st- TV cameras were seen in New York, California, Texas and most of the 50 states filming people in panic and people partying. Somber and happy people were in the same places. This continued into May 22nd then reality hit them. The somber were now happy and the party- goers were somber when they realized they were deeper in debt and possibly out of work.

May 21st came and went without any destruction. Clayton went back to see Dean.

"Dean, you had a lot of people worried. The preachers loved it, Church attendance was up by 18% last Sunday and most churches had the largest weekly collection ever. People have been calling the paper for an explanation. They would have played golf, if they had known it was all a hoax. The paper is really taking the heat from its subscribers for printing your prediction."

"Your readers must understand, I made a minor calculation error. The day of doom will be October 21st."

The Margarita Girls

The Margarita girls gathered the last Friday of each month to unwind over margheritas, a little food and more margaritas. Once a year they took a long margarita weekend to some place they had never been. A rustic cabin on the Tennessee River was their destination this year.

"Lois, get that sheet of directions out. We are almost to Decatur. Bonnie said as she put on her blinker and pulled onto the exit ramp.

"It says turn left and go about four and a half miles past the last public pier."

"How will we know the last public pier? We've never been here before. " piped Karla.

"Just wait a minute, Karla. Give me a chance to read all the instructions. Now where was I? Past the last public pier. Look for an old battered fishing/duck hunting boat on its side at the water's edge camouflaged with dried leaves and grass. A little further up there will be a bend, follow it until you get to the chert road down to the cabin. It is right on the water's edge. The key is over the door. You can't miss it. Enjoy your weekend"

Bonnie slowed down to a crawl after crossing the bridge. There was nobody on the road tonight. Lois and

Karla craned their necks looking for the water's edge through the scraggly trees and tall kudzu.

"We've gone about six miles, and haven't seen a pier yet. I'll drive just a little further and if we don't see a pier or the duck boat, I will turn around."

Karla winked at Bonnie then in a low quivering voice said,

"It's creepy with the kudzu covering everything like a mysterious creature with its arms outstretched with fringe hanging from its limbs ready to Grab Us! And its long flowing robe closing in on us at the sides of the road."

"Karla, don't talk like that. screeched Lois.

"Lois, Karla, look to your left. Is that big hump the boat with grass and leaves all over it?"

Bonnie didn't wait for their reply. She picked up her speed and drove through the narrow wall of undergrowth that covered part of the curvy, rutty road then slammed on her brakes. Lois lurched forward and hit her head on the windshield. Karla came tumbling over the front seat with legs flailing and glasses dangling from her nose.

Still laughing, Bonnie asked, "left or right?"

"It doesn't say!"

Bonnie instinctively steered to the left inching her way as she searched for the first road to the left. The pavement ended and they bumped along the chattering chert. Bushes scrapped against the side of the car down the winding path that seemed to be closing in on them then cleared at the water's edge. The sun cast a sheen on the water that seemed to ripple a hello to them. There wasn't a key above the door. Bonnie tried the knob and the door opened. This certainly wasn't how the cabin was described by the rental agent. Rustic was not the word for this cabin. Dilapidated was more like it. It was damp and chilly. They decided to scrounge up some twigs and dried wood from the wooded area around the cabin for the fireplace. Bonnie saw it first-the old weathered store sitting on the edge of a slough. She peeked in the windows. There was still food lining the shelves, a pot belly stove stood in the middle. The porch squeaked as she walked across and tried the door. She turned the knob, put her body against the door and pushed with all her might and it opened. She blew the dust off a mason jar of canned peaches. There were jams, vegetables and dried herbs that crumbled as she touched them. She closed the door and went back with her armload of wood.

"Where were you?" inquired Lois " We called but you didn't answer. I even tried to reach you on your cell phone, but we must be in a dead zone.

"You have to see what I found.

They jogged along the water's edge jumping over pieces of driftwood and avoiding the rusty beer cans that littered the shore until Bonnie pointed to the path that led up a rise.

"I went inside. It is like the owners left in a hurry, or died and just closed the door."

Karla crept into the store on tiptoes looking for snakes or other varmints to jump out of a corner while Lois and Bonnie looked at the rows upon rows of mason jars full of decaying food. Lois picked up a jar of canned green beans and noticed the jar behind it looked strange. It too had beans, but no liquid. She picked it up for a closer look and noticed the white edges of money behind the beans. She motioned for Bonnie and Karla to come over. Fearful that someone was near, she put her finger to her mouth so as not to speak and pointed to the money inside. All the jars on the second row were the same. Each had a few shriveled beans and a thick wad of money.

They moved a row of pickles behind the front row of beans and blew dust over the area where they took the pickles. They stuffed a jar in each of their jacket pockets, closed the door and hurried back to the cabin.

They closed the curtains and locked the door. With a pitcher of margheritas they sat by the fireplace and counted the money.

"It's $80,000! $80,000!!" squealed Karla

"This calls for another pitcher of margheritas." Bonnie said as she poured each a drink.

They emptied the third pitcher, and giggled as they showered each other with money.

Mr. Landry, the rental agent, lived across the river from the cabin they had rented. He became concerned when he saw no car and no lights in the cabin. He called the sheriff's department to see if they had been involved in an accident. They had not. He dialed Karla's cell phone, but couldn't get a connection. He called her home phone and got the answering machine.

"I'm not available right now. Leave a message and I will get back with you as soon as possible."

He called later in the evening and got the same message. Mr. Landry went to the local 7/11 store to get donuts. Deputy Bradford had just gotten off work and was paying for gas when Mr. Landry walked in the store.

The deputy turned and asked him, "Have you heard from the ladies who had rented your cabin?"

His jaws tightened and he clenched his fists as he shook his head no.

"I'm off duty, but I'll call into the station and ask them to watch for them on patrol. I'll ask that the water patrol also check along the river. "

The next morning sober, they decided to leave. They stuffed the money into a plastic grocery bag and put it inside the blender. Then put it inside its box. It was noon when they turned the car around and headed up the drive. A battered truck was coming down the drive. Karla dialed 911 as the giant man got out of the truck and walked over to Bonnie's window. Karla, the ditsy blonde, clicked on speaker phone and held the phone in her trembling hand on the seat, so the dispatcher could hear.

"Where do you ladies think you are going? "

"It is a little too chilly for us. We are heading back to the city. You can keep the rent for tonight Mr. Landry.

Bonnie said. "It was easy to find your place. Your directions said go to the left at the bend and it led us to your rustic cabin. We will have to come again in summer.

"The name's not Landry. What are you doing on my property?"

"We thought this was the cabin we rented. said Lois.

"I think you ladies know what I want. Back your car to the cabin or I'll push it back there with my truck.

They had traveled about a half mile on the chert road, far enough away from the cabin to have weak cell phone reception. The phone was on the seat and out of view of this gruff looking man.

The dispatcher could hear the conversation and motioned for one of the officers to come closer to listen, too. He nodded and two squad cars were sent in search for the women and the demanding man. Mr. Landry was called to find out if there were any other cabins in the area. He mentioned the abandoned store and gave them general directions.

They didn't turn on their sirens for fear that would alert the man who had stopped the carload of weekend renters. The deputies saw deep tire tracks leading down an overgrown road and slowly drove down the eerie twisting drive. From a short rise they could see the two vehicles stopped a short distance ahead in a bend in the road. One deputy's car was parked to block the road and the officers ran along the shadows of the overhanging kudzu. Before he realized it, the officers seized the giant of a man and tackled him to the ground as he tried to get away. Handcuffed, he tried to explain he was just questioning the group about why they were on his property. Karla held up her cell phone and the deputies said nothing. They radioed their location and said they had a person in custody.

Shackled, he was walked to the old store where the margarita girls showed them the jars that had held the money. Karla nudged Lois and kept looking back at the car. Afraid they might be arrested too, Lois told them of the blender of money they had taken from the jars and gave it to the arresting officers. A police van arrived and the jars were taken. Prints were taken as well.

All went back to the station for a report to be filed. Lois could hardly hold the wheel she was so nervous. Were they going to be charged with stealing? They were afraid to ask. They didn't want to give the officers any ideas. They were told they would have to stay in town for at least another day until they complete the initial investigation. They stopped at Wendy's and got burgers, fries and large soft drinks and checked in at the Holiday Inn. There would be no margaritas.

The Pinkerton representative was called. The $2.3 million dollars recovered was from a heist the year before. The thief is awaiting trial and his partner has also been captured and is behind bars. The Pinkerton Company gave the women the $100,000 reward money. They decided next year they will stay in a condo at a nearby beach where it is open and there are lots of people.

The Rough Looking Cowboy

His cowboy boots scuffed on the sidewalk. He wore well-worn blue jeans. The kind of well-worn look that only came from hard work. His oversized belt buckle let everyone know he was a fan of NASCAR. A container of smokeless tobacco was tucked inside the pocket of his white tee shirt. A John Deere cap protected his head from the bright sunlight of the streets of Fairhope. When he reached his truck, parked parallel along North Summit Street, he opened the door, looked both ways on the street, and reached his hand behind the driver's seat into a cooler. He pulled out a Bud Light and in a single motion twisted the top. He threw the cap into the truck bed without looking. In four swallows, he had an empty bottle. Again, he reached into the cooler, placed the empty bottle, and pulled out another beer bottle. He twisted the top and threw the cap back into the truck bed aiming at the other cap. He took one swallow, climbed in his truck, started it up, and headed for his appointment at the Eastern Shore Art Center.

He parked his mud-spattered truck across the street from the art center and just sat there for a few minutes. He took in the funky sculptures outside as he pulled out a wad of tobacco and put it in his mouth. He chewed on it for a minute or two, then dropped it into the well inside his bottom lip. He looked at the package beside him and the letter that went with it. He'd promised her he'd deliver it when the time came and now it was here. He climbed out of the truck, spat out the brown juices and tobacco, then headed for the front door. With a strong grip he swung the door open and walked up to the receptionist. A soft-spoken volunteer of advanced years, greeted him and asked if he was there to see the exhibit on Western Art. He glanced around as she motioned to the gallery to his left, but said,

"No, I have an appointment with the director of this art center."

His look was stern and his voice gruff.

"Just a moment while I ring her office. What did you say your name is?"

"I didn't", he replied a little annoyed.

Hand shaking now, she buzzed to the downstairs office. The phone just rang, but no one answered. She excused herself and walked down to the kitchenette to see if the director was having her usual lunch of cream cheese, crackers. and an apple. The director looked up and smiled at Hattie, the volunteer, and asked if she wanted part of her apple. Hattie said, "No, thanks". She stood there facing the director and said," I hate to bother you at lunch, but there is a rough looking man at the reception desk and he said he had an appointment with you.

"What do you mean 'rough looking?"

"He looks and acts like the villains in western movies only rougher, if you know what I mean. Should I call for security?"

"What did he say his name is? I don't recall having an appointment today with a man. I have one appointment this afternoon, but it is with a former student of mine. I taught her in a beginner's mixed medium class 10 or 12 years ago. She had potential and I hope she is coming to show me some of her work. I've got about 10 minutes until her appointment. Show the man to my office and tell Peggy to keep her office door open."

The elderly volunteer went back down the hall and to the reception desk, but he was not there. She peered into the gallery just in front of her desk, but didn't see him. She walked into the next room and still did not see him. Hesitantly, she headed down the steps to the downstairs gallery and saw him examining a wood carving. His look was softer. His hands held the piece like it was a fine piece of China. He set it back on its stand and faced her.

" The director, Mrs. Waters, will see you now."

Down the narrow hall she walked and he with his broad shoulders and clicking taps on his boots followed holding his brown paper package. He sat down in the tiny office and looked around. Mrs. Waters reached out her hand in greeting, but he just tipped his hat and said,

" Ma'am"

"You said you had an appointment with me."

"My name is Nathan Ritter and I am here for my wife. Her name is Reba. She was Reba Butler before we married about six years ago. Reba and I live in Idaho and travel the rodeo circuit. We were headed to Robertsdale for the yearly rodeo when we had the accident. She was hoping you still worked here. She said you gave her a chance and encouraged her to continue painting when she was down and out. She told me she lived here nearly a year and worked as a waitress to earn enough money to move to the west and the rodeos. That's where I met her. Spunkiest thing I'd ever seen with that flame red hair, green eyes and dare devil attitude. That's what I like about her most, but that is not why I'm here. Reba has been painting across America. Everywhere we'd go, she took her roll of canvas and her chest of paints and brushes. She's sold a few pieces when we were down on our funds and needed money for food and gas. There isn't anything she can't paint and they deserve to be in a gallery like this. Reba would have come herself to show you, but she was thrown by her horse last fall and has a broken neck. She can't use her arms or legs anymore, but she still wants to paint. She'd heard about people painting with their mouth and she has been trying really hard to do that. I promised her the next time I passed this way for a rodeo. I'd bring the pieces she thought were the best and give them to you. I cut a rough piece of wood to make a frame for the three she sent."

The rough and gruff cowboy looked broken and vulnerable sitting there while she unwrapped the pieces. Reba had captured it all–the grass swaying in the breeze, the snow-capped mountains, the herd of buffalo grazing in this rugged country. The shading, the shadows, the feathering strokes- it was all there. The director sat in disbelief. This was some of the best artistry she had seen in a very long time. She looked at the other two pieces, equally as remarkable, then she looked at him.

A smile had spread across that weathered face and he asked, "Are they good enough to hang in a gallery like this?"

She shook her head, smiled and shed a tear all at the same time. Composed herself and asked, "What is in the envelope?"

He handed it to her and she opened it and pulled out the artist paper with a water color drawing of her and scrolled at the bottom was "Thank you, Reba Butler Ritter". Now a director isn't supposed to cry nor a big, tough looking cowboy, but that day in that office they both did. Reba's art, all 208 drawings, paintings and water colors will be on display for the March Art Festival.

Aged, but Not Alone

It's time for a weekend away from the children now all teenagers. George and Ruth, Ed and I packed our overnight bags, told the kids we were off for a weekend alone. We would call them periodically to make sure they were still alive and that our houses were still in one piece. They looked at us in shock that we would go off without telling them where we were going.

We went the back way out of Birmingham up old US 11 through Dogtown and Collinsville, the backside of Fort Payne, passed the original recording studio of the singing group Alabama, then turned right to slowly take in the beauty of the west rim of Little River Canyon until we got to Point Rock. There was silence as we took in the view. Ed and I smiled and enjoyed the mountains around us and the gorge below us with its meandering ribbon of water. This site, created by nature, had changed little over time. The wind seems to whisper to us,

"Movement of plates 300 million years ago created this gorge and formed the Appalachian Mountains.

As the years passed, steam from 8 miles below the earth's surface built up until it bubbled to the surface on the mountain top and Little River was formed 1800 feet above sea level. For 53 miles the river meandered on the mountain top before dropping 500 feet into Weiss Lake and then a tributary of the Coosa River. It was the only river in the hemisphere that formed and flowed over a mountain top. The water contained no pollutants and flowed through the pristine wilderness."

This was a vignette of what awaited us further up the road. The road was lined with woods. People seemed to slow down almost to a crawl as they approached the park entrance. Wild flowers in spring, the undergrowth of the woodlands, said good morning, enjoy my beauty.

We checked in, got maps of the park, spoke to the park ranger about walking trails and about the falls, then rode to our chalet, Number 14. We had requested this chalet because from the back of it we could walk down a path to the water's edge. Possibly it was a path the people of the Cherokee Nation had used after making this vista their home. It had everything they needed. There was a source of water for themselves, for fishing, and hunting of game. The game would come each day for water. The Cherokee could wait, then kill only what was needed, then use every part of the animal. Caves, invisible to the naked eye, dotted the rock walls and were inhabited until permanent shelters could be built and in time of danger, they provided protection from their enemies. Flat land on the mountain top allowed them to plant crops. Along the water's edge, bits of shale and flint, the rock used to make arrows and spears, were found.

As we rode to the falls over the twisty road with outcrops of boulders everywhere and a canopy of trees overhead, Ruth read, then commented that de Soto Falls was named after the Spanish explorer, Hernando de Soto. He had heard of gold in the valleys and mountains of Alabama, Georgia and Tennessee, so he sent Lieutenants Siva and Vilebo with a small band of soldiers to find the gold. They traveled north of this virgin wilderness in both Georgia and Alabama and arrived at the rim of Little River Canyon on July 9, 1530. They were greatly impressed and made reference to its beauty in the historical account of the trip and described the beauty of the lofty hills and stupendous rocks; they saw the gleam of yellow rock and thought it was gold. Upon examining it, they found it was iron oxide instead. For at least two days, possibly longer, they camped at the falls. They searched for gems and gold each day and returned to their camp by the cool clear waters at the falls. They remained in the area until 1541 then traveled north when hostile Indians repeatedly attacked them.

My husband parked the car and we got out to a roar of water gushing over the falls. Eyes then feet turned toward the roar. The concrete steps brought us closer to the roar of the water as it cascaded over the dam. High rock walls before us on the other side of the falls had rock climbers repelling down the wall. It was a beautiful sight to see them swing out then bend their knees as they returned to the wall then spring out again. As we stood at the metal railing a spray of cool water washed over us and we could see that there were two falls. The first with water crashing over the dam wall, ran across a smooth rock surface then plunged several hundred feet to the Little River far below in the canyon. From this vantage point we could identify the birds in the trees, on ledges and circling overhead and were aware of the other creatures in camouflage watching us. Hunger pains had us returning to the car for sandwiches, chips and cold drinks as George and Ed pitched stones into the river to see who could create the largest splash. With full bellies we walked down the side of the dam, over the boulders of gray and red to the ledge where millions of gallons of water raced to the gorge below.

With walking sticks in hand, we hiked down the many trails until the sun waned and we headed for our chalet. Were these the trails the people of the Cherokee Nation walked? They had peace in this woodland with a few trappers arriving in search of pelts. Some stayed and married Cherokee maidens. Chief Sequoyah was the son of a Cherokee mother and a German Father. He was born in Tennessee, moved to Georgia, then to Alabama. He fought with Andrew Jackson and Sam Houston at the Battle of Little Big Horn in the War of 1812 then returned to his people. A brilliant man, he devised an alphabet and taught the Cherokee people how to read and write. He moved to Will Town in the 1820's and remained there until the Treaty of New Echato was signed in 1838 which turned over the Indian land to the federal government. Most of the Cherokee people did not want to leave their land. They understood the beauty of the land. They took from it only what they needed and always returned to the land what was Mother Earth's. The woodlands, mineral springs, fresh water, shelter, all nature's creatures to feed them, and a beauty were unsurpassed by any land they had ever seen. Why should they leave?

Some 1103 followed John Benge, a Cherokee brave, to other areas of North Alabama. Some hid in caves until the thrust to remove them from their land calmed down. The rest were forced to travel to Oklahoma. Though promised food, clothing and help with family, the United States Government did not follow through and many left their homes with few possessions and ill prepared for the long trip. One in seven died along the Trail of Tears. Had their journey started in these woodlands? Were the rustling of leaves and the chirping of grasshoppers we heard the same sounds they heard at night or was the whispering wind their spirits returned to nature? The chill of the night forced us indoors and the used energy of the day caused our eyes to droop and our beds beckoned us to rest.

The next morning, as we sat around the table in our robes drinking coffee and eating a hearty breakfast of homemade biscuits, eggs and bacon, we heard car doors slamming. We stopped eating, listened and shook our heads in disbelief as seven of our combined nine children came up the porch steps about the time George opened the front door. Laughing and holding large bags of Hardee's biscuits and cinnamon rolls, they trooped into the kitchen/living room and commenced to devour their food as we retreated to our bedrooms and dressed for the day. Part of the menagerie of teenagers took the trail behind the chalet to the water's edge. The path was narrow with a dense undergrowth of wild plants rooted in time and an umbrella of tall, aged trees hiding the sun. The rest of us began walking down the circle drive of the chalets. We all suddenly stopped and pointed to a tree in front of us. On one of the top branches of the tree were three possums hanging upside down with their tails wrapped around the branch. They played dead as possums frequently do and we continued our walk. We tried different trails, identified leaves and birds, looked at animal tracks, watched for snakes and bound across clear streams. In silence we watched a rabbit munch on plants, turtles creep toward the water, birds fill their bills with grubs and worms and saw a doe with her fawn scurry by on the path ahead. This was tranquility in nature.

With eleven hungry mouths to feed, we headed for the Log Cabin Deli in Mentone. The rustic restaurant is a half block down from the Mentone Springs Hotel and the White Elephant, a hodge-podge building of antiques and junk. The warm mineral springs of Mentone are but a short walk away. They were the main reason this community evolved. Visitors came for the healing waters and to enjoy the swimming, fishing and cool summer temperatures. The waitress seated us at the back tables encircled by windows. The area glistened like the windows with the warmth of laughter and talk while waiting for food. The meal was topped off with steaming hot peach cobbler and rich vanilla ice cream.

There would be one last stop before we sent the kids home and that was Sallie Howard's Memorial Chapel. Colonel Milford Howard, a self-educated entrepreneur, had built this chapel after his first wife's death on land he had purchased to build a master school for underprivileged children. But with only forty students the school could not support itself. Howard, who had only 11 months of formal education, did not want other children to lack for an education. Mostly on credit he bought 1000 acres of land. When the Alpine Master School failed, he tried to sell off the bulk of the 1000 acres to developers, but to no avail. He thought if he built a dam at the falls it would attract more buyers. Developers still were not enticed. He decided a highway from Chattanooga to Gadsden would surely bring buyers up Lookout Mountain. He completed the road from Gadsden to Mentone, but still the land didn't sell. He would not live to see its development into De Soto State Park. After his death, his second wife had him cremated and his ashes were placed inside the boulder that forms the back portion of the altar. The chapel has been maintained and weddings and sometimes church services are held there. In a quiet reverence our families went into the church, said a prayer, read the inscriptions and slipped out.

Down the trail from the chapel there is a stone patio, formerly a boat launch. Sometimes people bask in the sun in this isolated spot then take a cool dip in the river water, but not today. The bathers on the stone were coiled, patterned snakes, water moccasins. The teens stopped short of walking onto the stone boat launch covered with snakes. They turned and quickly came back to the cars and us. We said our goodbyes and the children left for home and we traveled back over the roads built by the Civilian Conservation Corp during the Depression. Men who signed up for six-month commitments to live in encampments and build roads, bridges, dams, fire towers, and work in rock quarries, plus many other jobs, were provided, housing, meals, education, recreation and work with an allotment of $25.00 per month sent back home to their families. They transformed that 1,000 acres of unsalable land of Milford Howard's into a state park being careful to keep its unique features unchanged.

As we drove back to Point Rock, we saw the fences, rustic cabins, trails and dams they built during the Great Depression. We also saw fewer trees, more houses and some erosion along the east rim of Little River Canyon. The clean waters of Little River are slowly being polluted. The Clean Water Act of 1992 has helped. Also, through legislation, the Little River Canyon National Preserve went into effect in 2001 to control pollution . This federal law states that this is significant scenery; therefore, twenty-three miles of preserve roads, two waterfalls and eight overlooks have been created to preserve the west rim, but other measures are needed too. The public needs to be educated about how to preserve the pristine woodlands and develop the east rim with conservation of the land paramount in future development. Scientists, educators, students and concerned citizens of the area are testing soil and water and monitoring endangered plants and aquatic life in an effort to restore and enhance the beauty of this pristine woodland with its deep gorge and one of America's purist rivers snaking its way across the mountain. Our car rolled to a stop and once again we are mesmerized by the majestic beauty before us. This virgin woodland is now preserved by federal law.

We will be back in the fall when the mountain is dressed in brilliant yellow, red, orange and brown leaves.

Happy

Every morning as I left for work, I saw him standing in his garden with a cup of coffee. I presumed it was coffee. He waved to all the motorists as they passed by. For years, I waved to him. He was always there, a bright moment in my day.

Meticulous beds of roses, yellow lilies and lavender painted the sloping lot. Bird feeders and bird baths added to the beauty. I wondered if he was out every day to watch the pecking order of the birds who occupied this sanctuary. Did he come to groom his flower beds or pick flowers to bring to his wife with her morning coffee? Did he have a wife? I'd only seen him. I could imagine all kinds of reasons for his morning ritual. I wanted to be like him, retired, enjoying my morning, and waving to passing motorists. SOMEDAY, SOMEDAY.

The morning paper said the house would be featured on the home and garden tour. I had to go. I had to know. I went early and parked my car on the side of the road below the gardens. I didn't want to be trapped by others and unable to leave and go to the next home on the tour. The tour was to begin at 10 a. m. and I had arrived at 9:33 A.M.. I walked up the steep slope, stopping several times to inhale the morning fragrance. Near the top of the crest, there was a flagstone walkway that led to a series of brick arches and a terraced area, then a circle driveway with a border of low red plants. From this vantage point, I could see the city below. It took my breath away. I just stood there for several minutes. The flagstone patio curved around the side of this simple stone home. I kept looking for Happy, for that is what I named him. Where was he? Maybe he was setting up trays of sweets, brewing a pot of coffee, or setting out vases of cut flowers from his garden.

The flagstone continued up four steps to another archway and a circular patio, an outdoor haven with tables and chairs facing the bluff that overlooked the city. The arched entrance was covered in greenery transforming from a lush green to a deep bluish-green.

I heard voices. I stepped back behind a large potted rose bush, and turned my attention toward the patio. Happy wheeled his wife to one of the wrought iron tables, then retreated to the house. He brought out a tray with two flowered China cups of coffee, I presumed, a matching plate of English muffins, and a single rose. He kissed her lightly, handed her the rose, then turned slightly and took the seat beside her. He handed his wife the muffin to eat as they listened to the chirping birds. She ate a couple bites then put it down and tugged at his sleeve as she pointed at a maze of morning glories.

In her broken speech, she said, Mornin' glories come bloom in June,"

She smiled at him as he squeezed her hand. He returned the smile, but with tears streaming from his eyes.

I slipped away down the path to my car. I'd not be touring the house. I'd seen the beauty of this home from that patio.

Determined to Give and He Gave His All

July 29, 1932 - A father died of pneumonia. His wife was six months pregnant with their sixth child. Life was very difficult with little income and few relatives to help his wife raise a family of seven. She and her husband had moved to America in 1912 to have a better life and raise a family.

When her youngest child was nine, his two brothers enlisted and served in World War II. His oldest brother returned to civilian life after the war and his other brother decided to stay in the military. He looked up to his brothers and wanted to serve his country, too. He was very tall with a serious older looking face and enlisted in the Army National Guard at age 14, I am told. I am not sure if that was allowed or if he lied about his age. When he turned 16, he lied about his age and joined the Army. He was sent home when the Army found he was underaged.

He was determined that he was going into the military. His mother pleaded with him not to join. There was a war brewing and she feared he'd be wounded or killed. Finally, his oldest brother, who was acting head of the household, signed the permission papers for enlistment. His mother, my grandmother, said her rosary all day, every day for the safety of her son in battle.

He went through basic training and learned his specialty as a field wireman with the 61st Field Artillery Battalion, Cavalry Division. He came home for a few days to say goodbye then his battalion went to Japan on its way to North Korea. While in Japan he bought gifts for his family members and mailed them home. I have the white silk scarf with an embroidered flower he sent for me and inherited the salmon-colored bed coverlet and clutch purse he sent my mother.

The 61stField Artillery Battalion fought fierce battles and some died. A typhoon struck the area during his last battle. A telegram was sent in July, 1950. stating he was missing in action. He was just 17 years old. In September, 1950, a few days after his 18th birthday, an officer came to tell my grandmother her son's body had been found. It was never clear if his body had been swept away by the flooding or under water for a period of time. My grandmother lost her husband on July 29, 1932 and her son born three months after his father's death in September, 1932, then 18 years later on July 25, 1950, shortly after the Korean War began, Private First-Class Costanzo Rogato died in battle. His mother was left with an American flag, the Purple Heart Medal and her memories. His name is engraved on the Korean Memorial at the USSA Alabama Memorial Park, Mobile, Alabama,

The Leather-Bound Book

Shay and Heather bought the old house at the edge of town and planned to make it a bed and breakfast when they retired in two years. There was much work to do to spruce it up. They fixed loose boards, changed plumbing, refinished the cabinets and floors. The first level of the house was almost ready.

The attic would be their next project. Shay lifted the door and pushed it back to the side, then he and Heather pulled themselves into the dusty dim space. Shay found the string and pulled it. The dim yellow glow revealed boxes and trunks everywhere. They blew the dust off a box and lifted the lid. It was a box of leather-bound books with cracks creasing the leather. Shay picked up one on family history. He crossed his legs and set the book in the well between his legs. Almost immediately he was absorbed in its content. Heather took many of the books out. She read the titles and thumbed through a few of the pages then put the books back in the box, stood, and looked around. She saw a dressing table near the window with something bulky on top. She showed her husband and he got up and moved boxes and furniture to get to the vanity. The bulky object was a book. Heather picked it up and said to no one in particular, "That's odd. Everything up here is dusty, but this book doesn't have any dust at all."

Shay had returned to the history book he was reading and Heather began to leaf through the bulky book they'd found on the vanity. She looked out the window and noticed it was dusk. Heather closed the book and looked for Shay. He had leaned back against a box with the book in his lap and fallen asleep. His wife gave him a nudge. He stirred, stood and stretched before climbing back down the narrow steps. They closed up the house and took the two books they'd found interesting home with them. They'd return to their 100 year home next week after they got off work. Every night that week they raced home from work, ate a quick supper and spent each evening reading from the books. Shay learned the original owners had built the house for their growing family. The vast plot of land had various farm animals, chickens, a milking stall and chickens roaming everywhere.

Heather said the book she was reading was very strange. It too had a date of over one hundred years ago. Shay asked what was strange about the old gray book. His wife shivered and read the title: Brew, Remedies and Special Powers for Those Who Believe. It had a diagram of an herb garden with each plant numbered. There was a description of the healing powers of each plant numbered. The next section of the book was titled "Brews". A glass with a swirl of smoke inside was underneath the title. The heavy coarse paper added to the mystique. The preface read: 'There are brews to keep. '

And brews to change your mood

Brews to cast spells

And spells to make you brood

Heather bought the herbs shown in the diagram and Shay built a raised bed in the backyard for the herbs. They spent the afternoon placing the herbs in the exact location as the diagram. As she picked up her tools and turned to the garden she said, "Grow a foot by next Saturday.

She believed the plants bowed their heads when she told them not to disappoint her. It was very eerie. They spent the rest of the afternoon pulling weeds, cutting the grass and planting wildflowers. All week Heather wandered around the city trying to find a fruit sieve. All the brews started with fresh fruit. Each recipe for the brew stated the fruit had to be ground until it was pulverized. The only sieve she found was rusty and lumpy. She used lemon juice and boiling water to remove the rust. Shay took a mallet and pounded out the dents. The instructions for the brew said to grate the rind of a grapefruit, an orange and a lemon. Add the juice of the grapefruit to make a paste then smear it on the joints that hurt and leave it for four days and your pain would be gone. Neither believed the pain would be gone in four days, but they smeared the joints to prove it was a hoax. For the first three days nothing happened, but on the fourth morning, the paste had cracked and fallen off. As Heather washed off the residue, she felt a strange sensation, almost a tingling. The pain was gone. Heather raced in the kitchen where Shay was making coffee and showed him how easy she could lift and lower her leg. He shook his head and said, "Honey, there are no such things as brews to make you well. She ignored him. She was beginning to believe.

Heather read the directions for the next brew. "Cut a leaf off each herb on the first row of your herb garden. Cut each leaf intro four pieces. Pour into a glass of warm water and stir six times. If you believe, the brew will turn blue. Drink it in one gulp then sit in the sun for an hour. To prove how silly these brews were and how silly she was to believe, her husband drank the blue liquid and sat in his lawn lounge chair for an hour. He'd fallen asleep as soon as he climbed in the chair. Exactly sixty minutes later, his eyes popped open. His hip did not hurt. She made other brews from the book and she especially liked the sleeping brew. Shay tried it too. He was beginning to believe. The tea mixture was very bitter, but she always was asleep in minutes. Their medicine cabinet was filled with salves and tonics she'd made for every ailment.

Heather now felt she was a master of the first three parts of the book. She was ready to learn the chants to create spells. She told the herbs to grow a foot when first planted and the next Saturday they were a foot tall. She remembered the book was on top of an apron when found in the attic. She washed it and wore it one day while making candles. She tied the wicks to their frame, melted the wax and began to pour it. They flopped over and she shouted, " Don't you dare! Straighten up. Before her eyes the wicks stood tall. The wax thickened before her eyes and hardened within minutes. On her next batch she told the candles to twist and they all began to turn. She had her old apron on another day when she dropped a vase. She reached for the broom and dust pan as she spoke. I wish vases could glue themselves back together and the pieces swirled into her vase again. The magic only occurred when she had the old apron on and she believed.

They put the leather-bound book and the apron in a chest in the attic and locked it. They hoped the spirit would stay in the locked chest, asleep as it had been before they found it. The brews were thrown in the gully that ran along the back of the property. Within weeks tall gray, thorny plants appeared and began creeping in the yard. A landscape company was called. They used a backhoe to pull up the weeds and planted trees along the water's edge. Daily they watched as the invasive plants smothered the trees and squeezed the life out of them.

They continued to restore the house, but found their work was undone each time they returned. New fixtures were found on the floor and the old was back in place. New wallpaper was in curls on the floor in the bedrooms and the old still covered the walls. New lamps were shattered. Only the original lamps found in the home remained untouched.

The house seemed bewitched. They thought if they got the chest with the book and apron inside, they'd get rid of the spirit. Shay and Heather climbed the narrow attic stairs and tried to lift the chest but it would not budge. They hired two men and the four tried to lift it. The chest was even heavier and they could not move it. The owners watched their efforts destroyed and realized this house wouldn't become a bed and breakfast. It belonged to the ghost who lived there long ago and still did. They locked the doors and put aside their dream. The thorny plants that had squeezed out the life of the trees near the gully continued to spread until they had covered the house and put it back to its ghastly sleep.

Sunset at the Pier

There is a special time of day when Mother Nature dims her light and signals young lovers, camera buffs and silver haired couples to migrate to the pier. Maybe a picture, a wish or a kiss is waiting there. The silver-haired lovers had done them all. There was a reverent silence as nature's camera clicked from scene to scene and usually, they anticipated the changes and delighted as each new stroke of color was added, but not this afternoon. She could feel his tension as they walked hand-in-hand down the pier.

"Want to talk?"

"You know what's bothering me, Baby. The damn blood sugars"

"Your ledger of readings and dosages didn't look out of line,"

"I didn't think so either, but he wasn't pleased and decided to tweak the dosage again. I didn't have this much trouble when I took the four shots a day.

They walked in silence, then stopped and leaned over the rail to watch the lemon sun of day dress and redress itself from goldenrod to a richer sunflower.

"Sorry Baby, it just seems the harder I try, the more problems we have to face with my health.

He stood there hunched over the rail in silence, sometimes shaking his head and balling his fist then relaxing it. She stood there beside him and waited. He had to work this out in his head before he could share. A fish jumped out of the water then plunged back as the brown pelican dove in after it and he remarked, "Did you see that!".

She nodded and smiled and he just looked at her. Time seemed to stand still, then in a very soft voice he said, " I shouldn't complain. There are others with heavier crosses.

Silently, he rubbed her back, then pulled her closer and gave her a peck.

"That was nice and the sun is just starting to set," she teased.

"Woman, I love you."

"You'd better, I've invested too many years in you"

With a half-smile they turned their attention back to the now tangerine sky and its glow softened his tension.

"Thank you." he whispered.

The minutes ticked away too quickly and the sun inched closer toward the horizon. The orange glows of the sun reflecting in the water seemed to add a glow to them as well.

He said, "I love it here. The sound of the waves lapping the shore and the sunset remind me of home and walking on the beach at dusk. If there were more than two people on Rehoboth, we thought it was crowded. "

There was a twinkle in those blue eyes as he reminisced about his youth, but they clouded over again.

The sun deepened its facial color to flame and appeared much larger and his taunt jaw seemed to relax as he asked, "Would you want to eat at the Yardarm instead of having to cook tonight?"

"Are you asking me out on a date?"

"Baby, you are more than my date and you know it. Come on woman, get yourself in gear."

It was early yet, and the Yardarm was almost deserted. They'd have the place to themselves.

"Come on in folks and find yourselves a table. Well, hello. I haven't seen you two in a couple of weeks."

"He has kept me slaving at the stove. I guess he was tired of my cooking tonight."

"Your favorite table on the deck is empty. That's two unsweetened teas, a hamburger plate and grilled shrimp over rice, right."

"You know us too well. Meals are correct, but tonight make it two non-alcoholic beers instead," he said as he motioned for his wife to go before him. They sat at the table closest to the boat slips. Their eyes shifted from the burning sun to the fluffy white clouds as they became saturated with color. There was total serenity in this spot as they watched the ducks weave in and out of the pilings, listened to the chatter of metal on the moored boats, and enjoyed nature's wonderland as it changed before their eyes. The ball of fire continued its descent until finally it deepened to ruby before ducking under horizon's blanket. As it slipped down to its bed, there was a crescendo of color above, and their eyes shifted to the light reflected off the pollution painting the canvas sky with layers of beauty. The tension he felt earlier melted away. Each stroke changed the character and awoke the striated garden of rose, lilac and lavender that glided across the sky as sailboats glided into their slips. Prisms of reflected light shimmered across the deep avocado water until darkness. The pillows of white, then pink transformed over and over again until the eggplant clouds rolled across the sky and shadowy reflections could be seen from their vantage point on the deck as they sipped beer.

He looked at the plate of rice and shrimp, mentally calculating its carbohydrate value, then punched in the numbers in the black monitor cupped in his hand and administered the bolus of insulin.

The final shafts of light rippled and danced across the waves ,then faded away as they consumed their food. Picking up his last skewer of shrimp he said, "At least they haven't taken shrimp and crab away from me yet."

They clicked their bottles of beer before downing the last of it and headed for the cash register. He paid the bill and inquired, "How does your grandson like college?"

As the owner counted out the change she smiled and replied, "He loves Alabama and seems to have balanced having fun and studying. He's a good kid and we're proud of him. Have a good night and come back to see us."

As he always replied, "You have a better one."

Strolling toward the parking lot, the only sound was the soft zing of fishermen cast their lines. Nature's majestic video had ended. Day was put to sleep and night was ushered in with a rich sapphire darkness. The pelican, the sentinel of the bay, perched upon the bleached pilings and kept watch over the ebony water. He leaned down and kissed her and said, "The sun is down now, Baby." He grinned and danced around to the driver's side.

My Dream Vacation

I have had many dream vacations in the past twenty years. My husband and I traveled to Hawaii. We spent a week in New Mexico for the balloon festival, basked in the sun at Rehoboth Beach, Hilton Head and West Palm Beach, seen the sights of New York and Washington many times. I've traveled to Italy twice. I've seen the beauty of Austria and Germany and lots of places in between. Alaska and travel by the Canadian Rail are two vacations I'd like to consider, if I had someone to travel with me. Maybe my Canadian friend, Anne, would be a good travel companion for the rail trip from ocean to ocean in Canada. An Alaskan cruise was a dream vacation Ed and I had planned for the summer of 2011 for our fiftieth wedding anniversary and his seventy-five-birthday. Without him, it has lost its luster.

Hawaii would be my dream trip. I've enjoyed the sites of Oahu and basked on the private beach area of the Hale Koa Hotel. I've shopped at the international market, been to the Pearl Harbor Memorial, traveled by air to National Volcanoes Park and walked on the hardened lava beds and looked up to see the glow of red cracks venting ash. I've walked through the dead lava tubes. I enjoyed my day and evening at the Polynesian Village and luau. I want to visit it again. A week was not enough time to see it all.

As I plan my next trip there, I think of the other islands that I did not get to see. I want to walk the green lush hills of Maui, listen to the sounds of birds and the roar of waterfalls. I want to go to the wild side of the island of Oahu and watch the surfers ride the big waves. I want to know what is on all the islands and the only way I can enjoy them all is to take a cruise around the islands. I would plan a two-week vacation. I'd fly to San Diego and spend the day at its zoo, then fly to Oahu. It would be my first and last stop on my vacation. I'd spend three days at each end of my vacation at the military resort in the heart of Oahu. I don't want to see the sights again. I just want to enjoy the resort. I'd board a cruise ship on my fourth day and spend seven days enjoying the good life of the cruise ship and visit each island.

I would again stay at the Hale Koa. I'd feel safe there whether traveling with someone or alone. It is a very up-scale resort for the military, their families and certain retirees from the Department of Defense. I'd ask for a room with an ocean view on at least the fourth or fifth floor. I'd have my meals there in one of its dining rooms. I'd spend my day on its private beach. I'd walk the paths through the gardens away from the water then have a cool drink by one of the pools. When I want another, I will hold up my glass and an attendant will come and refill it for me. Music plays and laughter and splashing of water as families play in the pools will fill my ears. If I want solitude, I will go to the adults only pool which is away from the other two pools and surrounded by tropical plants. I could read, sunbathe, lounge in the pool or take a nap in one of the beach loungers. In the evening I will dine at one of the dinner-theater shows, eat at the KoKo Café or at the Bilas and listen to all the different kinds of music as I dance the night away.

On a weekend night I will attend the luau on the grounds. I will walk with all the guests through the tropical gardens to the thatched hale (house). I will be shown how to make a lei and I will wear my floral creation as a roasted pig cooked in the imu or underground stove is served. Contented after a delicious meal, I'd have a fruit drink in a coconut shell as the fire knife dance and the hula are performed on stage.

Relaxed after three days of doing whatever I wanted, I'd pack my bags and ride to the port to board the cruise ship. I'd stand on deck and wave to the people below. I'd pay extra to have a water view from my room. I would request that I be seated at the Captain's Table on one of the nights I am on board. I will eat at the casual dining areas for breakfast and lunch, but want to dress up in evening attire and feel special every night. I'd end my evenings with a walk on deck with the stars and moon lighting my way and the wind kissing my skin and running its fingers through my hair.

The ship would anchor for two days at Maui. Each day after a hearty breakfast I'd meet our guide and travel to the lush green hills, climb the paths and walk under the waterfalls. There would be many paths to explore. A light lunch enroute of fruits and sweet breads would sustain me until the dinner meal. Each day would be a new adventure, a memory forever in my mind. Every island would be unique in its own way. I'd learn of the creation of these volcanic islands and the inhabitants who live on each.

My seven days at sea end and I return to the Hale Koa to relax and rejuvenate before coming home.

My dream vacation is just that anymore… a dream.

Was Thomas Wolf Right After All? Can You Go Home Again?

HOME IS A MEMORY OF WHERE YOUR FAMILY LIVED. When I was growing up that meant a community of about six thousand people. Most of the people in the community had lived there all of their lives and when they married, they stayed. The name of the community had changed several times from Green Pond, Cory and Fairfield. My great-grandfather started a family grocery store there nearly a hundred years ago. My grandfather initially worked for the railroad and then the tin mill before taking over his parents' business. My father bought the store from them in 1945 and my oldest brother became the owner in 1970 and operated the business until he retired. My brothers and sister and I attended the same schools as my uncles, my dad and my aunt. Many of my classmates' parents and my dad were classmates from 1920 to 1932.

In the early 1900'sthe Tennessee Coal and Iron Company (later known as U. S. Steel) planned the community around its industry. The city would have company housing, company stores, a hospital, and originally a one room school. It was a steel mill town. U. S. Steel dominated the area. Most men and some women worked for U. S. Steel. Some lived in the company duplex houses that were located on a hill across from the wire mill. There were two company stores in the heart of the city where workers could charge goods and food. The charges would be taken out of their next paycheck. Men who served in World War II were promised their jobs when they returned. Their families continued to live in the company houses. Some who served used the GI Bill to get an education and moved where there were good jobs.

Some dads didn't return home and some of my friends lived with their mother and at their grandparents' house in the community. Some mothers remarried after their husbands were killed during the war and continued to live in Fairfield. Few new students moved into the area when I was a child. I started and finished school with most of the same children.

All businesses except one drug store and the movie theater closed on Sunday. Most businesses closed at noon on Wednesday when I was a young child, many parents went to the park. Children played or swam in the summer months, that is until the polio epidemic. The pool was filled with dirt and covered with grass. People, afraid of the disease, quit going to the park. Businesses remained open on Wednesday afternoon after the scare.

I was a lucky one. I enjoyed the small community feel throughout my childhood. City Hall, the library and the supervised skating rink were all housed in the same building in the heart of the town and opened for several hours after school until it was supper time for most. Saturday at noon the movie theater had double feature movies which were appropriate for school age children. Cost was a dime. A few ticket numbers were called out during intermission and the ticket holder got a silver dollar. The theater was always packed. Children came and went everywhere without parental concern.

Most of the students of my era at Fairfield High School went to college. Many of the guys served in Vietnam then went to college. Many returned to the Birmingham area, but not Fairfield. Those living close by continued to go to the Baptist, Methodist or Episcopal Church in Fairfield or attended when visiting their parents. In May 2010 the Methodist Church had its last service. The church was packed, the outside of the church and the blocked off street was filled with members and former members listening to the final service over a loud speaker and joining in the singing of familiar hymns.

My husband and I moved back to the Birmingham area after he graduated from college. I would go to Fairfield to do my shopping even though there were shops closer to our apartment. We bought our first home on the other side of the county where my husband was teaching and which was nearer to the hospital where I worked. We had a family, continued our educations and worked. Our pace of life seemed faster. When time permitted, I would still go to the shops in Fairfield when I visited my family. Each time I went to my parents' or grandparents' homes, I noticed changes. My parents moved about five miles outside of Fairfield, but they still owned and operated their business in Fairfield. I didn't go to the downtown area anymore.

In 1987 we moved to Kentucky and my visits to my parents and other relatives did not take me to Fairfield. Sometime around the year 2000, my two older sisters commented about how much had changed in the past few years. The three of us drove through the business district with boarded windows and nearly deserted streets. Next, we went down Valley Avenue. The high school and the first elementary school we attended had been torn down and a new high school built in its place. The second elementary/junior high school was still standing, but was now the police station. It needed serious repairs. Lloyd Noland Hospital, where I worked during my senior year in the lab and which guaranteed me summer employment for two summers with enough wages to pay for my college tuition for my first two years, had been torn down. A gated fence blocked our entrance to the level ground being prepared for an extension of Miles College. The two-way street that led up the hill to what had been our childhood home and our parents' business was now a one-way street. The homes leading up the hill had been torn down and apartments built in their place. I didn't want to see any more.

Two years ago, a classmate and I met for lunch in Birmingham. After lunch, Sandy took me to Fairfield. We were both in tears when she drove through what had been beautiful streets with well-cared-for yards. Many houses had burned , a reminder of the drug making in the area.

Many yards were overgrown. Houses still occupied, needed repairs.

Times have changed. The steel industry has only a few hundred employees maintaining the many facilities, but no steel, wire, tin or coke plants operational. Many workers moved up north to other steel producing areas after many strikes. One strike lasted nearly a year. Repeated lay-offs and closed operations sent more men and women in search of work elsewhere. This continued until now empty eyesores stand idle and a town has died. The company stores closed a long time ago. Decaying company housing was torn down. Businesses unable to survive the tough times closed. First the A&P, then Food World closed. The hardware store and two drug stores closed. The movie theater was closed and left to deteriorate. The only family restaurant closed. The bank closed. The doctors in the family practice retired. No one replaced them. The downtown area has few businesses. The library, I am told, has one lady working and it has been her total career. The skating rink in the basement of City Hall has not been used in years. Walmart, located on the fringes of the city, closed about a year ago. Now there is no grocery store in the area. Walmart provided 45% of the city's revenue. Without it, Fairfield couldn't pay its bills. Public transportation stopped serving the area. There is no money to pay the police or firemen. The city asked to be annexed into Birmingham, but were denied. Now emergency services must be provided by the county which means great delays.

A teacher I had in high school commented at one of our reunions, " Don't go back. Life is never the same as you remember it. It changes as you have change with the circumstances that surround you. She was so right. The people who lived there and were educated there meet for lunch on the second Wednesday of each month. Sometimes stories of life in that community are shared, sometimes it is a speaker, but mostly it is the tug of the bond of that community that brings them together on the second Wednesday of each month at the Golden Corral in Pelham. I always try to plan my visit to Birmingham so I can attend these lunches with the alumni of many classes.

In answer to Thomas Wolf's question, let your memories serve as your visit back home.

My Favorite Place to Read

As I look out my kitchen window and glass back door, my wicker rocker beckons me to come and sit with the morning paper and a cup of hot tea. This old white wicker rocker with flaked paint and a broken piece on the rim by my head seems to say,

"Come, put the big fluffy green flowered pillows in my empty seat and find peace and solitude with me.

I answer that call and go to my open-aired sitting room, I call a back porch with its big gas grill, wicker settee, plastic lawn chairs and a beige and green outdoor rug that defines the space. To the right is a square glass and wrought iron end table. It is where I place the telephone and the newspaper as I finish each section. To my left is a mosaic tile round plant stand faded over time with a bit of rust, but it is the perfect size for my cup of hot tea or a glass of diet cola. Overhead a lighted fan provides a cool breeze on very warm days and it also tends to keep the bugs away. Above my head and to my left are four sets of wind chimes and each time I sit in my rocker they chime a hello. I say it is my deceased husband saying,

"Hello my love, I am here beside you.

From my vantage point, I can rock back and forth, listen to the birds, feel the wind gently brush my face and arms and cause my hair to dance. Traffic whizzing past, and an occasional barking dog can be heard. As I look out and around my yard, I see the green of some plants and the brown withered leaves of others. Yellow, white and purple pansies add color beside me as do the big clay bean pots of yellow mums. The camellias filled with buds are ready to burst open and frame my grotto that is home to my statue of the Blessed Virgin Mary. The bare trees and brown grass asleep for winter complete my haven separated from the outside world by my weathered privacy fence. I am alone with the newspaper or a good book. Periodically, I lay the book I am reading on to my chest, take off my glasses and just rock. Sometimes my eyes close to count the holes in my eye lids and I nap as the soft breeze and warm sun bathes me. As I wake, I see the fake rock on the wire shelf that has written on it "Every day is a gift of possibilities.

I smile, pick up my book and begin to read again. I am at peace with the world.

Ed and Jo Graven

About the Author

Josephine Graven, known to most as Jo, is the mother of four children, grandmother of six adult grandchildren, and one great-grandson.

Mrs. Graven attended Jacksonville State College in Alabama and is a three- time graduate from the University of Alabama in Birmingham with reading endorsements at the masters and advance certification(a second master's degree) in education. Her twenty-nine years of classroom teaching were in Catholic school, public school and military dependent schools. Jo served two additional years as administrative intern for the assistant superintendent of curriculum at Fort Knox Military Dependent Schools. She was a Kentucky trained mentor teacher for first year teachers.

Jo was twice recognized as Elementary Teacher of the Year for the Tarrant City School System in Alabama and represented the school district for Jacksonville State University Teacher Hall of Fame. She is listed in Who's Who Among American Educators and Who's Who Among American Teachers. Ms. Graven has been a member of Delta Kappa Gamma International Society for 25 years and has served as president of a local chapter in Kentucky and twice in Alabama. She is a past president of the Lincoln Heritage Reading Council in Kentucky.

Mrs. Graven was a co-recipient of a Kentucky Center for the Arts Grant. Jo has given workshops in educational curriculum and storytelling at the local, district, state and southeastern conferences.

Ms. Graven has written for her alumni quarterly news booklet for over ten years. She has authored two seasonal cookbooks and co-authored a third cookbook. Jo is a storyteller who writes most of her material. She was a member of Tale Talk and E.A.R.S. storytelling groups in Kentucky. Jo is a member of Story Jammers storytelling group in Baldwin County, Alabama. She was one of four Gulf Coast storytellers featured in the Mobile Bay Magazine in 2012.

Made in the USA
Columbia, SC
21 October 2021